Jonathan B. Mann

The Life of Henry Wilson, Republican Candidate for Vice-President, 1872

Jonathan B. Mann

The Life of Henry Wilson, Republican Candidate for Vice-President, 1872

ISBN/EAN: 9783337402884

Printed in Europe, USA, Canada, Australia, Japan

Cover: Foto ©Raphael Reischuk / pixelio.de

OF

HENRY WILSON,

REPUBLICAN CANDIDATE FOR VICE-PRESIDENT,

1872.

BY J. B. MANN.

BOSTON:
JAMES R. OSGOOD AND COMPANY,
(LATE TICKNOR & FIELDS, AND FIELDS, OSGOOD, & CO.,)
124 TREMONT STREET.
1872.

Rand, Avery, & Co., Stereotypers and Printers, Boston.

PREFACE.

THE remarkable career of Henry Wilson would justify a much more elaborate and serious work than would answer the purpose of a political campaign; and such a work, it is understood, has been undertaken. Although Mr. Wilson is more generally known than almost any public man of the time, and known to have been a long and consistent advocate of certain liberal radical ideas, that, in practical politics, commenced working in this country since he came upon the stage, and which have won their way to a success so grand that they are not to-day found liberal enough for the men who have uniformly opposed them, yet the best informed minds are little aware of the full nature and extent of his labors and influence on behalf of these ideas, or of his interest in, knowledge of, and powerful advocacy of, many other and highly important matters of legislation and public concern.

He has been so long in public life, and been such an intense, continuous worker, and so prominent in those causes that have most excited the people, that men have lost sight of labors and acts of his sufficient to have made the reputations of scores of public men who might have performed them as a specialty. Notwithstanding his long, able, and consistent career in advocacy of measures and principles no one dares now to dispute, notwithstanding his large-hearted sympathy with the poor, the oppressed, and the ignorant, and notwithstanding a life of devotion to their interests, there are those who pretend to regard his nomination to the office of Vice-President of this republic as anomalous, — the result of a lucky or unlucky accident, — and who would raise doubts of its fitness. With a view to place within the reach of such the materials for forming a sounder judgment of the man, we have been tempted to give in a plain way the story of his life as it is.

It is not claimed that he is faultless; but his mistakes and errors have never been seriously injurious to the State, to mankind, or to any of the causes in which he has been prominently engaged. He has been emphatically a man of the people; and, as such, we invite for him an inspection of the record.

On the occasion of his silver wedding, Oct. 27, 1865, one of the editors of "The Springfield Republican," (liberal!) who knew him long and well, was constrained to utter the truth in fashion thus: —

"A silver wedding claims a silvery verse;
And Wilson well deserves a poet's lay:
But I in humbler measure must rehearse
How fairly earned the honors of this day.
For friendship here puts on more public guise:
The man *we* love has been the people's friend:
Not wedded faith more sacred in his eyes
Than Truth to champion, and the poor defend."

NATICK, MASS., Aug. 1, 1872.

RESIDENCE OF HENRY WILSON, NATICK, MASS.

LIFE OF HENRY WILSON.

CHAPTER I.

Birthplace. — Condition of the People. — Apprenticeship. — Early Aspirations and Struggles. — Freedom.

HENRY WILSON was born on the sixteenth day of February, 1812, in the town of Farmington, N.H., — a small town located in a deep valley through which runs the Cocheco River, a small but rapid stream, that, lower down at Rochester and Dover, affords extensive power for manufacturing-purposes, and from the latter place is navigable to the ocean for small vessels. In 1812, sixty years ago, Farmington was a new country. It had been a precinct of Rochester, and was incorporated into a town only fourteen years before the birth of Wilson.

It is a rough, rocky, broken country; and even now, a few miles out of the principal village, is still new comparatively; many of the houses being only the first remove from the log-cabin of the wilderness, — little low buildings with two rooms and four windows, an outer door at one corner, and rough shingling, unpainted, indicating moderate resources and the absence of most of the luxuries of modern civilization. In 1812, when it was all new and a wilderness, when the village proper was composed of a dozen houses, and the nearest approach to a town was Rochester, eight miles distant, and every thing raised on the land must be hauled to Dover, eighteen miles away, to find a market, the times were necessarily hard, money was scarce, and privileges were few. The people were poor, worked hard, lived on little; and only a few of the most industrious, economical, and lucky could expect to amass a fortune large enough to save their children from a life of similar deprivation and drudgery.

Winthrop Colbath, the father of Wilson, was among the poorest of the poor men of this then undeveloped and poor country. His father and grandfather had been poor men: and brought up as he was, with the family ideas all associated with extreme poverty as their only lot; shut out from the world of enterprise; ignorant of what the world was doing, and how it lived; deprived of opportunity to change his condition by the circumstance that the day's wages must be used for the day's sustenance, and the former never able to quite keep its heels from being trodden on by the latter under the best conditions, — there was apparently no incentive and no chance to rise in the world; and to such as he the case was hopeless. He grew up with no thought of much better things than had fallen to the lot of his progenitors. They had seen want all their days; their best efforts for two generations had failed to conquer the difficulties of the situation; the most favored people around them were gaining but slowly with all their advantages: and the choice lay simply between starving to death and almost starving to death; and that was all there was to it.

This extreme poverty of the family had its usual effect. It killed hope utterly in the mind of Winthrop. His every footstep was dogged by necessity. He expected no improvement, and adapted himself to his manifest destiny, trusting to obtain from contentment that happiness which never could reach him by any probable supply for the wants of civilized man. This degree of poverty has probably led to the invention of a current story in relation to the origin of the family, which appears to be without foundation. The only approach to a definite statement concerning this story, which the writer could get at, was this: Mr. Smith Colbath, a second-cousin to Winthrop Colbath, met a distinguished lawyer of the State a few years since who knew all about it; and his story was, that the original Colbath came to this country with an only child, a daughter, in the service of Gov. Wentworth, and remained on the place to take care of it when the governor was driven away by the people.

But this story cannot be true. It is entitled to no consideration whatever. Wilson's ancestors, on his father's side, were Scotch-Irish. They came to America from the north of Ireland early in the eighteenth century, and settled at Newington, near Portsmouth, N. H. Wilson's great-grandfather, James Colbath, grandson of the first settler, did business in Portsmouth from 1750 to 1783, when he removed to Middleton, in Strafford County, where he died, in the year 1800, at an advanced age. He left eight children, — five sons and three daughters. Winthrop, one of his sons, the grandfather of Wilson, settled in Farmington, where he died at a very old age.

The maiden name of Henry's mother was Witham, also of a poor family, and with general surroundings similar to the family she married into: so that, on both his father's and mother's side, there was not much for the poor boy to look back to but the history of hardship, want, and their usual attendants and concomitants. Their reputation, however, is simply that of poverty and obscurity, and not of crime; and they struggled to hold their own, but under peculiar and aggravating disadvantages. They were people of strong natural powers of mind: and the whole treatment of Wilson by his mother shows a degree of appreciation of his ability remarkably just, and a consistent, persistent effort to have him rise in the world; which, under the circumstances, proves her to have been a woman of great sense and discretion, and governed by a worthy and generous ambition. Those who knew her well say that Wilson inherits his moral and mental characteristics from his mother; while in stature, and physical form and feature, he bears a striking resemblance to his father.

The birthplace of Wilson was on the Rochester road, one mile below the village; but all traces of the habitation were long ago obliterated. Across the road at the foot of the knoll on which the house stood is an old well, over which is the well-remembered curb and sweep; but the "oaken bucket" has yielded its position to a modern tin pail. Four handsome elms adorn the highway on the same side with the well. Soon after the birth of Henry, his father moved to a small house one mile lower down towards Rochester. This house was standing twenty-five years ago; but the depression left by the excavation for the cellar, and the slight embankment around it, one or two domestic trees, and a little extra luxuriance of the grass, are all that is left to denote that it was ever the site of anybody's house. In the rear, at a few rods' distance, is a meadow watered by the overflow of the river: there is a forest in front; and far to the north-west, through the upper opening of the valley, Mt. Belknap is a prominent object against the clear blue sky. It was nearly all forest about the house in Wilson's boyhood. Henry was the eldest of a family of eight boys, who followed each other into the world as rapidly as the course of nature consents, increasing the cares and burdens of the struggling couple, and adding to the chances of starvation, which were sufficiently threatening before the advent of each new-comer and competitor. At ten years of age, Henry found an opening for usefulness and hope by being bound to service with Mr. Knight, a farmer near by, from whom another boy had run away for more congenial employment; and thus and ever afterwards he became self-supporting.

Just prior to this happened one of those little turning events which seem to control and shape the character and career of the individual.

While he and another lad about the same size were engaged in a boyish scuffle in the sand-bank by the roadside, Mrs. Eastman, wife of the village lawyer, came riding by, and stopped to reprimand the lads for their foolishness. She asked if they could read; and the eager manner of Henry, as he replied, impressed her very strongly that the boy she was reprimanding was above the common; and at once she promised to give him a book if he would go to her house and get it. He promptly went, obtained the book, and at the same time the privilege of going to Squire Eastman's, and reading his whole library of books and newspapers. This book was a copy of the New Testament. Mrs. Eastman was a sister of Levi Woodbury, governor of New Hampshire, Van Buren's secretary of the treasury, and justice of the United-States Supreme Court; and she possessed her full share of the talent of a remarkably talented family.

Her first impressions of Henry were confirmed, and more, by a further acquaintance. She interested her husband in the youth; and both kept watch of him, encouraged his visits to their house, advised him about books, and loaned them to him; and in all suitable ways stimulated his love of knowledge, and gave it proper direction. The son of Hon. N. Eastman, George N., who succeeded to the profession and business of his father, remembers how Henry, when a boy, would come to the office and discuss politics and literature, history, &c., with his father, in a way that only one or two men did; and his father and mother were always predicting a distinguished career for him.

Mr. Knight was a farmer who had got a start in life, and was doing well; but thrift in farming at that day implied early rising, immediate attention to the first thing in hand, adherence to the order of business through the day, strict watch of all the loose ends, and a careful economy of time and money. This was the fashion; and the importance of it was recognized by him, and never lost sight of. There was work always. When it stormed, there were tools to repair, harness to toggle up, corn to shell, threshing to be done, and various other things to keep the hands from loafing or fishing; and, when the day was over, boys and men were usually tired, and most of them glad to go to bed. It was not the practice of working farmers to light up evenings to read and talk; but the blazing logs in the open fire-place gave light enough for so much recreation of this kind as the wearied limbs would permit. But Henry had an excellent constitution; could endure more work than most boys; and, when the family retired, he would remain behind in the chimney-corner, and read till the last flickering ember gave up the ghost, and no longer could be punched into a spasm of combustion for his benefit.

By the indentures that bound him to the service of Mr. Knight, he was to enjoy the privilege of attending school one month in each year. Think of it, ye gods! A young man crazy for knowledge, absolutely crazy, and limited to one month of school per year, and such a school! Will that boy ever be a senator of the United States? Perhaps. He went the first day of the term; and the teacher marked for him a lesson in Murray's "Abridgment of English Grammar," — a lesson which, at the rate of three per week, would have taken him through the book in about a year. But Mr. Knight construed the contract so as to permit the schooling to be taken when there was least work, snow-storms, and weather too cold for out-door operations; and hence the next day of his appearance at school was three weeks from the first. Now, many boys would have forgotten their lesson in that time, had they learned it, especially as it was a lesson in Murray, which no boy of ten probably ever understood. But not so Henry. Called up to recite, he kept on past the mark, and on, and on, until the thing began to grow tiresome to the teacher, and he had to inquire rather nervously where it was all to end. His astonishment may be imagined when he was informed by the lad that the whole book was committed, and he could repeat it word for word from beginning to end. For a boy who worked during all the hours of daylight, and was a stranger to the invention of candles, this is about as good a feat of that kind as is recorded in history, we imagine. And so he went on for eleven years, receiving twenty-six days of instruction in each year, scattered along at unequal intervals, of the quality of instruction afforded by the period. But his devotion to books and work gave no time for sprees and larks: so the world is deprived of even a single hatchet-story to enliven these pages. Going to school in that way, he could hardly be said to have schoolmates; and all of them whom we questioned could think of nothing peculiar about him save his devotion to books, and an inveterate disposition to take the part of the "under dog in the fight." No small boy could be walloped by a big boy, when Henry was about, without his taking a hand to restore the equilibrium.

He had a great longing for newspapers: but as this was before the days of reading-rooms and institutes, and the mail came to Farmington but once a week, and only a few families took the papers, of which Mr. Knight's was not one, he was obliged to gratify his desires in this direction by getting his mother to borrow the weekly "Dover Gazette" of a neighbor after it was a week old, and the new one had come to relieve it from duty; and he would run home and read it at night, so as to have it returned immediately to the subscriber. And so he toiled for knowledge, and imbibed it and democracy actually on the run. Mr. Eastman had some volumes of newspapers carefully filed away in perfect order, — "Niles's Register," and some later Washington paper, — which he devoured; and there were Plutarch's Lives in his library, a memoir of Napoleon, and a biography of one Henry Wilson, whose character made such an impression upon the youth, that he resolved to be called by the same name, — a resolve that he carried out on attaining his majority.

When about fifteen years of age there appeared in "The Dover Gazette" a sharp criticism of Marshall's "Life of Washington," which was denounced as a bad book for having convinced some one that the Democratic party was in the wrong. "The Gazette" was Democratic. Here was a new idea, — the Democratic party in the wrong! Impossible. But then such a book should be seen. There must be curious things in it, — preposterous probably, and lies maybe, but yet worth looking at. But how to get it was the question. There was no copy in Farmington; and the first penny of the many dollars required to buy it had never yet found its way into the pocket or hand of this toiling and truth-seeking boy. After much inquiry, he heard that some marvel of fortune in Rochester village was the owner of this wonderful book: and Rochester was seven miles away; could only be reached by him on foot, and after the day's work was done. He must go for it and return, making fourteen miles, and then restore it and return, making twenty-eight miles on foot and in the night. True, he could send by some one for it; but the messenger might not half perform the errand, and he would not be sure of it: or it might be stolen from his wagon going or returning; and such precious freight as a book must not be trusted to chance travellers or careless clod-hoppers who had no idea of the value of books. So there was nothing to do but go for it; and he went. This was the way knowledge was disseminated, forty-five years ago, among boys born poor and in the country. Is a boy who earned it in that manner to be laughed down or sneered down by young gentlemen in kids, swinging their flexible rattans, and assuming all the graces of learning because of their knowledge of popular drinks and fashionable neck-ties? We think not. But Henry stored knowledge away for use; and at the age of twenty he could give the place of every battle in the Revolution and the war of 1812, the date, the numbers engaged, the killed, wounded, and prisoners on each side: so you could not ask him a question relating to these facts that he could not at any time answer.

With all his craving for knowledge, Henry could buy no books. The exigencies of the family prevented his father from giving him any spending-money; and as Mr. Knight made it a principle to spend none, and his contract did not require him to furnish any to the boy, he got none. Once, when there was a holiday, a farmer offered him a cent to dig out a stump that was in the way; and he took the job with alacrity, it was so exhilarating to be doing business on his own account. The contract proved heavier than he thought it would be, and the whole day was consumed in removing the stump; but he put it through nevertheless, and at the close of the day received his pay promptly in cash as stipulated, — the first money he could call his own. It was small pay; but what matter to a boy that was to become a senator? He might go to the Capitol round by that stump as well as by any other. It was a beginning, at least; and the cent earned as that was could not be foolishly squandered. He learned in that day more of patience and self-denial by far than he would had the pay been ten dollars in lieu of ten mills; and the lesson was more valuable than the dollars ten thousand-fold.

And thus he lived and worked and studied until his twenty-first birthday came and set him free. He now engaged work on the farm of Mr. Wingate for some months at nine dollars per month; and, when that time was up, he sought employment at Great Falls, Dover, Newmarket, and vicinity, at very small pay, willing to work for nine dollars per month, but unable to obtain even that small pittance; and he a stout, robust, healthy, full-grown man, in the prime of his powers, and afraid of nothing. His compensation for the eleven years' services with Mr. Knight was one yoke of oxen, value unknown, six sheep, and such knowledge of farming as Mr. Knight possessed, which, however valuable, proved insufficient to justify him in writing a book of instruction on the subject for the benefit of mankind. His services with Mr. Wingate yielded some forty-five dollars: so that at twenty-one years and a half he was fairly started with an available capital in cash value of less than a hundred and fifty dollars. But he had read more than seven hundred books, and more newspapers than any man in town at that date. He had a remarkable memory, especially for facts and dates; and, in reading, made a point not only to fix the principal incidents in his mind, but the precise time of their occurrence. This practice improved his memory; and afterwards the great stores of facts treasured away in his head, with no very definite purpose other than to possess knowledge, not knowing exactly when or where it might be used, became immensely valuable to him, and have made him a competitor in debate, that shallow and pretentious men have not been swift to encounter in the United-States Senate or elsewhere. So his worldly capital was not to be despised, after all.

CHAPTER II.

Starting out in Life. — A Tramp to Natick. — Apprenticeship. — Debating Society. — Abolitionism and Labor Reform. — Working. — Seeking an Education, &c. — Misfortune. — Return to Natick.

SOMEWHERE about the year 1832, rumors reached the slow and unprogressive region of Farmington, that in Massachusetts there were chances to obtain work at almost fabulous wages; and a few young men in and near Farmington had struck out for this golden land of promise to test the truth of the encouraging reports. Some of these had gone from New Durham to Natick, Mass., there learned the trade of shoemaking, and early in 1833 had returned and established the business at home. One day, young Wilson walked over to New Durham for the purpose of forming an engagement to participate in the advantages of this flourishing trade. The managers were very polite, and spoke highly of the prospects of the business, at the same time offering to impart a full knowledge of the craft to the adventurer for two years' service as an apprentice. To a young man who had already served an apprenticeship of eleven years of the most exacting toil, and who had just enjoyed the luxury of wages for a few months, the proposition was appalling; and he turned his back upon the establishment at New Durham, disappointed, if not discouraged. On his way back, the thought came to him that he might do for himself what these Durham folks had done for themselves; and he at once resolved to take up the line of march for Natick, and trust to fortune and his own exertions. On the second day of December he packed his scanty wardrobe in a bundle, tied it up with a cotton handkerchief as was the custom, cut a straight hickory stick by the roadside, and started on foot for the promised land, just a hundred miles by the nearest way, every step of which was taken without once turning back or faltering. He passed down through Dover, Salisbury, Newburyport, Lynnfield, and Charlestown, to Boston. At Lynnfield he called at the house of a Quaker and asked for a night's lodging. Before retiring he proposed payment in advance, which the good "Friend" was not disposed to accept in advance, as implying a distrust of the honor of his guest; and

Wilson was obliged to explain, which he did by saying he wished to be on his way before the family would be up on the morrow, and would not like to disturb them to settle in the morning. A few years after this he met in the legislature of Massachusetts, as a fellow-member, a son of this Quaker, who remembered the circumstance, because of the pertinacity with which the young pilgrim insisted upon advance payment of his trifling bill. When he approached Charlestown, the sight of Bunker Hill aroused his patriotism; and though very tired, and so foot-sore he could scarcely move, he went a mile out of the way for the sake of standing on the battle-ground of the Revolution, and seeing the spot where the destiny of the world was changed, as he had read in history. Passing through Boston under the shadow of the State House, little dreaming that under its dome he would ever be an actor in any capacity, he threaded his way out to the Neck, and in Roxbury began to inquire the road to Natick. The person of whom he inquired was not perfect in his geography, and pointed to the Dedham turnpike as the direct road; and so for ten miles he tramped on in the wrong direction. At Dedham his mistake was corrected; and he pushed on for Natick, but lost his way, and went by the Upper Falls, Grantville, and West Needham, arriving at the premises now owned and occupied by Hon. H. F. Durant, the distinguished lawyer and philanthropist, but then occupied by a shoemaker, whose hands were at work by candle-light, it being nine o'clock in the evening, and very dark. Wilson went into the shop, told the men how he had come from Dedham, was on his way to Natick, and wished to go to that part of the town where he could find M. Luther Hayes, an old Farmington playmate. One of the men knew Mr. Hayes, and informed him that it was five miles to his shop, and he still on the wrong road. This man, Mr. Sabin Felch, procured a lantern, and struck off across fields and woods to the other road, a mile distant, guiding the wanderer to the true way: and about midnight he reached Penniman's Tavern, on the Worcester turnpike; and, too tired and lame to go on, he went in and staid the remainder of the night. These details of the journey are given to show the obstacles which, at a date so recent, the young men at that time had to encounter, and with what indomitable pluck and perseverance they were met and conquered. They were a part of the education of the man; and his experience thus acquired taught him the advantage of not shrinking from difficulties, and not giving up the battle until victory is assured, or defeat unavoidable. The lovers of economy, and they who complain of board at hotels where the charges are five dollars per day, will be glad to know that the entire personal expenses of young Wilson on this expedition were a dollar and five cents; and yet there was not, and never was, a stingy drop of blood in his veins, as all who know him will abundantly testify. But he was determined to get on in the world; and, while his mother was suffering for the necessaries of life, it was no time for him to be spending money for luxuries or articles that he could well enough do without. He must get a start; and the first cent and the first dollar were essential to the getting of the first thousand.

In the morning he found his old Farmington friend, Hayes; interviewed him to ascertain what he knew about shoemaking; and before night made a contract with one Legro to serve him five months to learn the art and mystery of the craft as then understood and taught in Natick. So his trifling hundred-mile journey had enabled him to see Boston and Bunker Hill; had saved him a year and seven months' labor demanded by the wily New-Durhamites; and, what was yet a profound secret, had started him on the road to the United-States Senate and the vice-presidency of the great republic. Mr. Legro, to whom he was now apprenticed, was an intelligent and worthy man, but one who held more strongly to the philosophy and practice of contentment as an aid to happiness than the doctrine and practice of exertion. He was a good workman, pleasant, and faithful to his obligations, but absolutely in no hurry, and fully determined never to chafe at any defect of speed in the ordinary or any other rate of progress; and therefore the team of Wilson and Legro did not pull evenly together. At the end of three weeks, Wilson offered terms of dissolution, which were accepted; and, for the small sum of fifteen dollars, he was once more free, and possessed with some knowledge of the art of shoemaking, and more of the arts of shoemakers, was ready for a new departure. He now engaged a good workman to give him instruction by personal, exclusive attention for one month; Wilson to pay his own board, and the other party to receive the pay for all the shoes both should make.

At the end of this month his mechanical education was complete; and ever after he was able to take work on his own account, and received the current price for the goods which were in demand at that time. He now moved into new quarters; and the good lady where he boarded, years after, spoke very kindly of him, but said he would keep her from sleeping o' nights by the noise of his everlasting hammer, which was going all night. He could now earn his board and twenty dollars per month, and more by extra work at night; which extra was sure to be performed. And still he was not content. The location was two miles from the post-office and church: it was hardly a settlement, there being in the neighborhood only a half-dozen small shops, and no particular attractions in the way of society or prospective improvements. Altogether was it inadequate to meet the demands of one in such an intense hurry to get on in the world. The rewards of labor, compared with Farmington, were immense: but there seemed to be "room higher up;" and, in the autumn, Wilson took his earnings, and left for New Hampshire, where he invested them in poultry and other country-produce, which he brought to Boston market, and disposed of at a price which did not more than cover expenses and the original outlay. As he had made a careful calculation of the profits of this speculation in advance, the result astonished him; and any glimmerings of fancy that he was destined to be a great merchant were effectually driven from his head by this experiment.

He now returned to Natick, and engaged board with Deacon Coolidge, who lived near the centre of the town, where now is a large and thriving village; but then there were not more than a dozen houses all told. The selection of this house and family was very fortunate to Wilson in many ways.

The deacon kept the town library in his sitting-room, — a small collection of fifty volumes, perhaps, which had been published a long time, and were all regarded as standard books; though not exactly the fifty books Starr King was wont to say contained all that any man need to read. Rollin's "Ancient History," Robertson's "Charles V.," "Life of Charles XII.," "History of the Late War," "Vicar of Wakefield," &c., were the chief works; and they were read with eagerness and appreciation. The deacon had an excellent wife; and they received him as one of the family, and made him feel entirely at home; and it was one of those clean, quiet, regular New-England homes that to get into is a good substitute for a fortune. The influences were not only all good, but it secured a passport to the best society the village afforded; and the young boarder was appreciated by the head of the family, and encouraged in all his efforts at improvement.

The family had extensive connections in town; and, later, the influence of all was ardently given to assist him in his political ambition and schemes. In the immediate neighborhood lived a few ladies of great intelligence, and a dozen of young men near his own age, who were given to study, and greatly interested in all questions of moral improvement and the then vital topics of the time. To find so many young compeers with clear heads, correct habits, and honorable ambitions, was a great and agreeable surprise to him: and he had not completed the circle of their acquaintance when the thought of organizing them into a society for mutual improvement suggested itself; and he immediately began to talk up the scheme, and take measures to secure its accomplishment. The idea was favorably received. A little finessing secured the use of the district schoolhouse for meetings; and on the 30th of June, 1835, fourteen young men assembled there, and formed the Young Men's Debating Society, — the school that first gave Mr. Wilson an idea of his powers, and the opportunity and training that ultimately insured his entering into public life, and enabled him to maintain himself in the positions he filled. His improvement as a speaker was rapid and continuous; and he very soon, by his ability and application, assumed the undisputed leadership of the society. Many of the debates were memorable for the skill and power with which they were conducted, and are mentioned to this day, among the residents of the place, as events in the history of the period. One of the peculiar characteristics of Wilson in these debates was the intensity of his earnestness. He was active in securing the selection of live questions: and, if it fell to his lot to be designated to maintain the side not in accord with his convictions, he would procure a substitute if he could; failing in that, ask to be excused, or persuade one of the opposition to exchange with him, so as not to allow himself to argue against his own convictions. He could get up no feeling on the wrong side; and without feeling he could make no speech, and was always defeated.

The year 1835 was a remarkably bad year for abolitionists. They were mobbed far and wide in Pennsylvania and other States, and there were few localities where a public speech in favor of their principles would not bring the author's head into close relations with unsavory missiles. But these young men were, with about two exceptions, radical abolitionists: and, to the intense disgust of all citizens supposed to be in their right minds, they would have the question discussed; and, more aggravating still, they always would manage to have the weight of the argument on the unpopular side. It would come so, and there was no help for it; and, in the coming so, Wilson was a leading agent. The father of Mrs. Lydia Maria Child was a resident of Natick; and his distinguished daughter spent much time with him, taking great interest in the young men, and converting them, to her extreme doctrines. Her influence was potential; and the next spring, when Wilson made his first visit to Washington (a visit he has often described), he saw slavery with a conscience enlightened by the suggestions and arguments of that earnest and distinguished woman; and all his convictions were intensified, and turned into resolves.

These resolves to oppose slavery to the bitter end he has faithfully kept, and the cause has never once been hazarded or lost sight of during his whole career.

The elevation and improvement of laboring-men was one of the leading topics often under discussion at the meetings of this society, and among members in their social and casual intercourse. They gave it constant prominence and continued study; and, as a matter of course, Wilson was an ardent advocate of the rights of the workman as against all rival or opposing interests. As workmen in Natick and vicinity worked usually by the piece, or could if they chose, a limitation of hours by law was not agitated; and, wages being good, strikes were not thought of. Oppression there came in other forms, — in political and social ostracism. Standing in society was determined not by a man's merits, judgment, knowledge, and moral worth, but by his acres, stocks, and family. To change this was the problem; and it was determined to make Natick the first battle-ground, to be extended as circumstances should warrant. But, to gain an advanced standing, obviously the first requisite was to be qualified for it. This was attempted by reading, thinking, questioning, debating, writing, and seeking the most cultivated and intelligent society. The next point was moderate self-assertion in public affairs. In New England, town-meeting is public affairs; and when Wilson and his associates tried their little experiment of having the nobodies lead off in town-affairs, instead of following the somebodies who always had led, there was great consternation in fogydom, and great railing when the experiment succeeded. Since that day, arguments and character have been able to meet dollars and dunces; and mechanics have had it their own way in town whenever they have acted with sense and discretion. The first move was not for office, but in favor of improvements in schools, roads, methods of conducting business, and so on. The young element made itself felt immediately; and shortly it was the dominant influence in all public matters of a municipal or political nature, and made Natick one of the leading towns in Middlesex County, giving it a power far beyond its numerical strength, and a weight to which, on the score of property, it was never entitled.

During all this time, work was never neglected. Every week a given number of shoes must be turned out, and that number must equal the efforts of the most industrious. If the Debating Society took three hours of the time of an evening, some other evening of the same week must be prolonged three hours. The deacon's dingy shop had lights burning, in winter, till twelve o'clock, or later, most of the time; and the skaters were tired out and in bed, usually, long before the thumping of Wilson's hammer ceased to annoy the slumbers of the people in the adjacent house. At the expiration of two years and five months, he had made and received pay for six thousand pairs of shoes; and was the possessor of more than seven hundred dollars in cash, all his own earnings. But his physical system had given out; he raised blood, and there were unmistakable signs of exhaustion which he could no longer ignore: so, accepting the advice of Dr. Kittredge, he rested two months, and prepared for a term at school.

He was now twenty-four years of age, and only ready to begin a school-education; but, undaunted by nothing, he started for Strafford Academy, N. H., and remained there and at Wolfborough and Concord Academies for several terms, teaching district schools in the winter. The failure of a friend to whom he had loaned his earnings obliged him to abandon his purpose of perfecting an education; though a chance friend, Mr. S. Avery, took such an interest in him, that he offered to board him gratis so long as he chose to remain at Wolfborough and pursue his studies. In 1834 he returned to Natick absolutely penniless, and obliged to ask credit for a suit of clothes that he was greatly in need of; but the credit was of short duration, and they were paid for the moment he could earn the money.

CHAPTER III.

Manufacturing. — Political Discussions. — Entering upon Politics. — Marriage. — Election to Massachusetts Legislature.

SHOE-BUSINESS was now greatly depressed; work was scarce, and prices so low that Wilson decided to become his own employer, and try his hand at manufacturing. He purchased leather enough to make a single case of cheap brogans; made them with his own hands; took them to Boston, and exchanged them for leather and a small sum of cash with the firm of Jonathan Forbush and Co., wholesale dealers on Blackstone Street, and one of the heaviest houses in the shoe-trade. This operation proved somewhat better than working for a boss; and, adding a hand to the business on wages, he soon was ready for another trip to Boston with two cases, and the next time with three, until at length more hands were engaged, the stock increased, and in less than a year he was manufacturing on a considerable scale, and adding moderately to his worldly goods. He bought some land, built a shop, and in 1840 a house on Central Street, not far from his present residence.

The Young Men's Society continued its operations; and Wilson returned to it with increased zeal and enlarged ideas and ambition. At the academies in New Hampshire he had met in debate the picked young men whose talents had encouraged them to seek a liberal education; but in his old associates, the mechanics of Natick, he still found sufficient ability and skill in polemics to make it necessary for him to study and exert himself in order to maintain his ascendency. Indeed, he found them abler, on the whole, than the boys at school. Politics were raging, and these young men were intensely political. Late in the fall of 1839, a young man, Mr. Herring, who had recently moved to town, and a flaming Democrat, engaged in an animated talk on politics at the store where the post-office was kept, and where all political men met at mail-time to get their daily papers; and, finding each had more to say than could be said at such times, Mr. Herring challenged Wilson to a public discussion of the principles and merits of the two parties, Whig and Democratic. As no proposition could have more completely met Wilson's wishes, it was accepted with unconcealed satisfaction and alacrity: the arrangements were made at once, and the debate entered upon at the earliest practicable moment. It was largely attended, and immense interest was excited; it being the first actual political encounter of the kind in this part of the country. Mr. Herring was a man of considerable talent, but not so thoroughly posted as his antagonist, and with far less experience in debate: so the result was a discomfiture, which he acknowledged with commendable frankness, and attributed, not to the want of merit in his cause, but to his deficient presentation of it. He proposed, therefore, to substitute another party to continue the discussion; and, this being acceded to, arrangements were made for a meeting in the Methodist church on the evening of March 20, 1840, between Henry Wilson of Natick for the Whigs, and Joseph Fuller of Framingham, chairman of the county committee, for the Democrats, to canvass the merits of the two political organizations. The preliminary excitement was great; for politics had been increasing in interest, and the nation was standing on the very verge of the great upheaval of 1840, the most memorable merely political campaign this country has ever experienced in its whole history. At the appointed time the champions appeared, ready for the great conflict, and excited by the momentous interests supposed to be at stake in the discussion. An account of the debate appeared in "The Boston Atlas," written by an eye-witness, which we give below:—

EXTRACT FROM A LETTER IN "BOSTON ATLAS," DATED MAR. 21, 1840.

"Last evening was the appointed time: and at an early hour the meeting-house was filled by the farmers and mechanics of the vicinity, all eager to witness the mighty conflict.

"The meeting being called to order, Mr. Fuller rose, and stated there was some misunderstanding between them about the subject; that he had come to discuss the effect of the Sub-Treasury Bill upon the currency, while Mr. Wilson had come to discuss the currency question in general; and, this being the case, he did not know exactly what to say.

"Mr. Wilson said he had furnished his opponents with eighteen written charges against the administration; and, if they did not understand the question, it was their own fault. After some desultory remarks, Mr. Fuller said, if Mr. Wilson would go on with his argument, he would reply to his general remarks as far as possible, and to the Sub-Treasury part at any rate. Mr. Wilson then proceeded in a masterly speech to demonstrate that the government possessed the power, and was in duty bound, to furnish the country with a sound and uniform currency; that all the presidents, from Washington to Van Buren, had acknowledged the power, and acted under it; that the United-States Bank furnished such a currency; that Gen. Jackson, when he put down the bank, reconciled the people to it by promising a better currency: that the deposit bank system caused an over-issue of bank-paper, furnished the money for and stimulated speculation, and was one of the main causes of our late trouble; that Webster and others foresaw and predicted the result, which the administration denied; that this system is now repudiated by the same party; and that the Sub-Treasury is brought forward as the great financial measure of the administration, which he objected to, as proposing no relief to the people, as tending to crush the banks, destroy the credit system, and reduce the wages of labor and the value of property. In this connection he commented on the speeches of Calhoun, Walker, Buchanan, and Co., with just severity for their 'flagitious' avowals, and wound up by an appeal to all no longer to put faith in an administration which had broken so many promises, and never fulfilled the tithe of a solitary one.

"Mr. Fuller now rose, and said that it was somewhat late, and he was not fully prepared to answer all the arguments of his opponent. He was happy to state, however, that he was not opposed to banks or credit or the laboring-man: and he was very happy to inform the audience that the Sub-Treasury would have none of the doleful effects ascribed to it; that it would not affect the currency at all; it proposed nothing of the kind; it was simply a bill to provide for the collection, safe-keeping, and disbursement of the public money; and he would ask his antagonist to point out the section which proposed to cut down wages, ruin the country, &c. He expected his opponent would have taken the bill section by section, and stated his objections to each in particular; but, as he had not done so, he should leave the question, — it being late, — and his remarks, he supposed, were not very interesting. These are his remarks almost *verbatim et literatim;* and this discharge of the 'big gun' has had the effect of scattering the Locos like a flock of wild-geese in a whirlwind. They acknowledge another total rout, but promise to try once more, and intimate their intention of going to Boston to get a lawyer to come up and whip the Natick cobbler."

The next discussion was on April 3, at the same place; the Democratic side of the question being sustained by Hon. Amasa Walker, then a merchant in Boston.

A little incident occurred at this meeting, which, trifling in itself, added considerably to the prestige of Mr. Wilson as a careful and strong debater, — one who, as the farmers say, "put up the bars" on leaving the field.

In order to avoid a misunderstanding like the one at the previous meeting relating to the terms of the question, Wilson furnished his opponent with the form of the question in writing: "Is the financial policy of the past and present administration beneficial to the country?"

Mr. Walker in his speech made no allusion to this question, but presented an argument in favor of a pure metallic currency, which was not then proposed by the administration, and had not been, though strongly advocated by Col. Benton, and believed in by many Democrats.

To help Mr. Walker out of his predicament, the gentleman who had arranged the debate, and on whose behalf Mr. Walker appeared, rose and read the question as presented to him by Mr. Wilson, which was in a form to relieve Mr. Walker of his difficulty, and remarked that the original was at home in his "t'other jacket-pocket."

The account in "The Atlas" states that the original proved to be in the jacket-pocket of Col. Chester Adams, chairman of the meeting, who produced it; and it was found to correspond exactly with the statement of Mr. Wilson, and hence Mr. Walker was not extricated quite so cleverly as they had anticipated. It was one of those little blunders which faulty memories will cause sometimes, and which inure to the benefit of matter-of-fact men who have a habit of putting things in black and white, and securing the evidence of third and responsible parties.

Mr. Walker complimented Wilson highly for his ability and courtesy; and the two parted with mutual respect, and have been good friends from that time forward.

These publications in "The Atlas" attracted attention in the vicinity. "The Boston Post," with characteristic stupidity, in absurd conflict with its pretended respect for laboring-men, and regard for their welfare and advancement, called him derisively the "Natick cobbler;" and, thus advertised, he was soon an object of interest, and in demand at the log-cabin gatherings, which were becoming frequent, and affording unusual chances for the display of patriotic and youthful eloquence. Speakers were rare: but the demand was inordinate; and a mechanic who could stand on his feet and talk for an hour was not only a wonder, but a wonder of the right kind, and received with hearty appreciation. The public assemblies of that day craved two kinds of speeches, and seemed never to tire of either: humorous anecdotes and pungent facts were in equal demand; and Henry Wilson was a walking dictionary of facts, which he dealt out with such accuracy, with names and dates, extracts and proofs, so formidable, that contradiction was preposterous without counter facts and proofs; and these were inaccessible to most speakers, and therefore impossible. When a hundred items were given, the denial of one or two only appeared ridiculous; and Wilson had such an armory, that no man could follow him *seriatim*, and bring any thing in support of the counter-case.

The result was conviction; and large numbers of mechanics were led to abandon Democracy, and vote for Gen. Harrison for president, through his exertions. He spoke at Needham, Roxbury, Medway, Framingham, Concord, N.H., and numerous other places; and was everywhere received with enthusiasm, and listened to with profit; and he established firmly a reputation as a successful campaigner. The campaign concluded in November, 1840, by the election of Harrison to the presidency, and his own election to the House of Representatives of Massachusetts as the member for Natick.

A few months prior to the election, he was united in marriage to Miss Harriet M. Howe of Natick, a young lady of excellent mind, intelligent, amiable, and beautiful, but whose early loss of health and vigor prevented her taking the active part in society that she was fitted for. Nevertheless, she made many acquaintances in Boston and Washington, where she was highly respected; and died, after a lingering and painful illness of several years, in May, 1870, deeply lamented by all who knew her. Their only child, Lieut. Hamilton Wilson of the army, died in Texas in 1866 at the age of twenty.

Although during this whole season Wilson was absent from home, addressing public meetings, and attending conventions of his party, he kept his business well in hand, and succeeded, as the phrase was, "in doing well." His fame as a speaker caused many men in the trade to seek his acquaintance; and some of the most wealthy and eminent houses in Boston, New York, and other large cities, were greatly interested in him, gave him orders, and showed him attentions that were not only pleasant, but of great benefit. He was invited to their houses, and made acquainted with their experiences, and thus was taught to avoid dangers in the way of a beginner in business, and encouraged to hope for a prosperous business-career. His capacity for business was more than respectable; it was ample: and nothing but an all-absorbing devotion and aptitude for public affairs prevented him from taking rank as a man of business.

For ten years Wilson was actively

engaged in manufacturing shoes, producing from one thousand to two thousand five hundred pairs per week, chiefly adapted to the Southern trade; for Wilson, though an abolitionist, did not doubt the honor or honesty of the Southern people, and was not averse to having the bondmen properly shod. One of his customers who had failed, and promised to compromise by paying fifty per cent of the indebtedness, but proposed to raise the money in part by the sale of his slaves, received from Wilson a full discharge of the whole debt, and was requested never to send any dividend unless it could be done from money not obtained by the traffic in human beings.

As a manufacturer Wilson was enterprising and wide-awake, and let nothing but politics and philanthropy divert his attention from business. He sought for the best workmen; paid the highest market-prices for work freely, without grudging or grumbling; and was generous and fair in all settlements of disputes which always arise between manufacturers and workmen regarding the quality of work and the price which should be paid for it. There were no lawsuits on these matters, and no quarrels to disturb the peace of the village, or furnish food for scandal. He was just in all his dealings, stood to his agreements, and was popular with all who had occasion to do business with him from first to last. His political principles concerning the rights of the laborer he carried into business; and was never guilty of preaching abolitionism to the South, and oppressing his own workmen.

CHAPTER IV.

In the Massachusetts Legislature.

THE appearance of Henry Wilson in the legislature of Massachusetts at the session of 1841 was the beginning of a new era in the politics of the State. There had, it is true, prior to that time, been in the legislature many mechanics, farmers, and laboring-men of great ability, who had done honorable service, and won for themselves a highly-respectable reputation, but no one of breadth, force, and persistency sufficient to impress upon the State policy his own distinctive trade-mark, or to become a power in affairs necessary to consider in movements of importance, or capable of adding any thing to the prestige of the State in the greater theatre of national politics. And whatever may have been the ability or the opportunity or the promise of any young man coming from the ranks of the common people, and asserting himself, or assuming a position in affairs, there was a prevailing sentiment among those who held the leadership that modesty was a highly-becoming virtue, which, assiduously cultivated, would surely and rapidly make of such a one all that he need become. The atmosphere about the State House was so pervaded by this opinion, that young men were very likely to be anxious to find the status which would meet the genuine approval of our first men; and certainly none of our first men would be likely to see it anywhere near the front, or where crowding would be an inevitable result of a departure from the true and well-defined line of commendable modesty.

The advent of Wilson was the commencement of a new order of ideas on this subject; and, whilst he was well received and generously treated by some of the old managers, there were not a few who regarded him as a man sadly out of place, without the ability to maintain even a respectable position, and destined to an early and disgraceful obscurity. But this was an under-estimate of the man altogether, and is so confessed. He has steadily advanced in reputation and influence, and so easily passed many of those who at first thought him of too little consequence to be despised, that they have never been able to understand him or themselves.

During the first session of the legislature Mr. Wilson was constant in his attendance, making himself familiar with the routine of business, and sufficiently undemonstrative and retiring not to arouse the jealousy of any who might be disgusted with a zeal not according to knowledge. He merely did enough to let it be known such a person was there, and was holding to views that were sound as Massachusetts regarded soundness.

In the autumn of 1841 he was re-elected, and commenced his second term of legislative duty on the first Wednesday of January, 1842. At this time business was much depressed in New England, and, in fact, in all parts of the country. Importations were very heavy; money was scarce; the people were without employment; wages were low; and, though we were in that blissful state that goods could be had cheap, there were vast numbers who could not partake of the boon, not having the wherewithal to buy. Wilson was placed upon the committee on manufactures; and they were instructed to report upon the cause of the depression of business, and its cure, — a duty which was assigned to Wilson on account of his well-known interest in whatever concerned the question of work and wages. He made an elaborate report, accompanied with resolves, which met general commendation, and won for him a marked distinction. We were then at the lower end of the scale of reduction of tariff duties, under the compromise scheme of Henry Clay enacted nine years before. This was a concession to the threats of the free-traders; and, instead of the universal riches that were to flow in under the provisions of the vaunted revenue-tariff and low duties, there were great depression and prostration of business, much suffering, and general complaint. Though the logic of the free-traders was as unanswerable as it is to-day, it was somehow painfully apparent, that, under the free-trade system, the millennium had not come in; and in a time of general and profound peace, with the old national debt all paid, and the country in the full enjoyment of the happy financial schemes of the Democratic party, the government had to borrow the money to meet its current expenses.

Wilson in his report took ground that free trade was a failure: it did not fulfil its promises; and a revival of business could only be assured by a new tariff on the principle of specific discriminating duties. The revenue-tariff theorists alleged that duties could be laid for no purpose but revenue; and the tax must be laid upon every article imported, according to value. Wilson argued that this would be an actual discrimination against the poor, and in favor of the rich; and a violation of the just principle of taxation, which requires property to pay its proportion. Take tea, for instance, and subject it to an impost duty: as the poor man's family consumes as many pounds as the rich man's family, the poor man will pay the same tax that the rich man does; and, as the number of poor men largely exceeds the number of rich men, revenue from tea will largely fall upon the poor. But this was not all the injustice: for all the tax levied on tea would be taken off of something else, — off some article of domestic manufacture; and then the reduction on that article of domestic manufacture would enable the foreign manufacturer to come in and supply our market with the same goods, thus cheating the poor man of his chance to raise the money with which to buy his tea. A tax on tea, therefore, throws the burden upon the poor for the benefit of the rich, and compels the laborer, in effect, to pay a bounty to the foreign manufacturer, by which he is able to come in and deprive the laboring-man of work. That is, the tax on tea, if levied on articles which can be produced in this country, would exclude a portion of the foreign goods, the making of which would then fall to the operative here. Discriminating duties, hence, are necessary to protect labor from being discriminated against; and the argument was so clearly put, that the Democrats on the committee, after making a sophistical argument in favor of a revenue-tariff pure and simple, were compelled to assent to the principle of discriminating duties, though the two positions are in direct conflict. When you discriminate, it is in favor of something or somebody; and the principle, once admitted, overthrows the horizontal theory altogether.

It was also argued that our people are all consumers, and a majority are producers; that apparent inequalities are thus harmonized or equalized; that what we as consumers pay extra for in higher prices of goods we consume is made up to us in higher prices of goods we produce, — to all who produce; and, as it is the rich who do not produce, the share not made up to them is divided among the producers. The tariff, in consequence, inures to the benefit of the producer; and the producer, in all cases, is the man who labors. The tariff, by checking importation, gives the laborer employment; employment brings wages; wages enable him to buy and consume; buying and consuming create demand; demand makes business good; and good business makes general prosperity. The influence of the tariff on diversifying labor and stimulating invention, the mutual dependence of producer and consumer, and other points, were stated with a clearness that commanded great attention, and won for Mr. Wilson a meed of praise rarely awarded to a young legislator. The resolutions were such as Wilson can stand by to-day, and were as follows: —

"*Resolved*, That a division of labor by which the people sustain and support each other is indispensable to the prosperity of this Commonwealth.

"*Resolved*, That discriminating duties levied upon the productions of foreign labor tend to create a diversity of employment among our own citizens by enabling them to pursue occupations they would be compelled to abandon if brought into direct competition with the cheap labor of Europe.

"*Resolved*, That duties upon foreign imports may, without injustice to any section of the country, be so assessed as to encourage our diversified pursuits; and no policy can meet our approbation which does not guard with parental care the interests of the laborer, and promote his prosperity.

"*Resolved*, That productions are the result of labor; and any policy which seeks to cheapen products by encouraging the importation of such commodities as we produce tends to embarrass our laboring and producing classes by diminishing their wages and suppressing their employments.

"*Resolved*, That the time has now arrived when the exigencies of the government and the interests of the people demand a radical revision of the revenue laws; and we regard it as the imperative duty of Congress to encourage domestic industry by the assessment of specific and discriminating duties.

"*Resolved*, That our senators and representatives in Congress will consult the interests of this Commonwealth and the wishes of their constituents by using their best endeavors to carry out the views contained in these resolutions."

The abilities of Mr. Wilson as a practical statesman, and his devotion to the cause of freedom and the welfare of laboring-men, made it an object for the Whig party to put him on the senatorial ticket for Middlesex County in 1843; and he was one of five gentlemen who bore the honors and insults of this occasion. The county had been Democratic, and this year the people failed to make choice; but the Whigs, having secured a majority of the legislature, filled the vacancies by electing the Whig candidates; and, soon after the two houses were organized, Wilson was installed as a member of the Massachusetts Senate, and made chairman of the Joint Standing Committee on the Militia. The militia in the State, owing to the long peace, neglect, and the heavy expense attending drills, had been at a low ebb, and its use had come to be doubted by the tax-payers; and its honors had not been sought with eagerness by that portion of the people who could afford the expense of wearing them, and by others scarcely at all.

Wilson was too well posted in history and in the knowledge of human nature to trust implicitly in the appearances favoring a long-continued state of universal harmony, and for some time had interested himself in military affairs; had joined the volunteer military organization; had been elected major, then colonel, of the Middlesex Regiment, and subsequently brigadier-general of the Third Brigade; and was warmly in favor of reviving the military spirit in the old Commonwealth. As chairman of the committee, he now made a strong effort to revive the military organizations in the State, to secure enlistments, to promote the drill and efficiency of the various companies, and put the whole system on an honorable and permanent basis. To this end he drew up an able report and bill, with provisions to meet the main objects he had in view, and designed to distribute more equally the burdens of expense in equipment and drill to which the young men of the State had been subject.

This was the first serious movement toward that preparation for war which enabled Gov. Andrew, seventeen years later, to astonish the nation by sending to the defence of Washington the first fully-equipped troops, whose presence, perhaps, saved the capital of the nation from the hands of the insurgents at the commencement of the civil war.

In 1844 he was re-elected to the Senate, and maintained his standing as a wise and able legislator, and made some gain in the confidence and esteem of the leaders of public opinion; but, in deference to a prevailing rule which confined the term of service of a senator to two years, he declined a re-election in 1845, and was nominated and chosen to the House from the town of Natick.

The election of James K. Polk to the presidency, and the annexation of Texas, had so strengthened the proslavery party in the country, that the expediency-politicians were ranging themselves generally on the Southern side; and some of those who had been true to the better sentiments of the Whig party were greatly depressed in spirit, and inclined to regard a further contest as useless. How far the re-action had extended was not known; and whether any of the old leaders of the antislavery sentiment would be returned to the legislature in the House was uncertain. It was certain, however, that, without leaders there, the cause would be a sufferer; and the town of Natick resolved to prevent, if possible, the occurrence of such a contingency. Wilson was chosen at this election with special reference to the slavery question, and for the purpose of insuring the continued agitation of the subject at the State House, and preventing the retrograde movement from proceeding further.

The sentiment of the people of Massachusetts, though sometimes dubiously expressed, was always opposed to slavery, and in favor of such action as should curtail its power, and cripple its energies. This was always the opinion of Henry Wilson: and he believed not only in the absolute righteousness of the antislavery cause, but in the policy of incorporating it into the political creed of the party to which he belonged. It was the fashion in 1837 and 1838, at the conventions of the Whig and Democratic parties in the counties, to pass resolutions of a mild type in favor of freedom, the right of petition, and in opposition to mobs; and even Mr. Hallett, who afterwards became celebrated as the great resolution manufacturer of the Democracy, used at that period to draught sympathetic resolves to catch abolition votes. But later, as the crisis tended more strongly to a head, it became evident that the General Government was under the control of slavery; and that the Democracy, who were responsible for the administration, would be compelled to sustain it, or dissolve. Two courses, therefore, were left open to the Whig party: namely, to go counter to slavery, make a direct issue, and attract to its banner the spirit of freedom, of progress, and of the nineteenth century; or fall back upon the ideas of the dark ages, and run a race with Democracy for the Devil's influence and co-operation.

At this point a third party arose, called the "Liberty party," based on the idea that any effective opposition to slavery politically must come from the disintegration of the old parties, and the combination of their materials into the new organization. Wilson thought the body of the Whig party was sound on the question, and that the whole power of its organization could be carried against slavery whenever the test could be directly applied; and his desire was to work with the instrument already made, rather than try to make a new one.

In 1841 he and his old comrades of the Debating Society, and a few other kindred spirits in Natick, held frequent consultations in the shoe-shop of George M. Herring, now of Farmington, N.H., where plans, principles, prospects, and duties were discussed, and the incipient action taken which resulted in the movement afterwards known as "the conscience Whig party," of which Charles Francis Adams, Sumner, Phillips, Hoar, Allen, Palfrey, and Wilson were the leaders. This was a small beginning, much like the commencement of Wilson's financial schemes when he worked all day for a cent; but it was a beginning, and came to something in time. It was decided that thereafter no men should be chosen delegates to any Whig convention from Natick who were not in active accord with the proposed movement; it was decided to consult with the leading Whigs in all the adjacent towns, and secure their co-operation in the same object as regarded those towns; it was decided among them to write articles for the press in favor of the object, and to secure control of "The Norfolk-County American," which was in the market, and use its columns to promote the cause; it was decided that the influence of the Church should be obtained so far as was proper; and, finally, it was decided to organize the sentiment of the party in the State by securing the names of such influential persons as could be obtained in behalf of some definite course of action. These decisions were all carried out. Rev. Samuel Hunt brought the slavery question into the conference, and secured desired action. Another of the active members of the *coterie* purchased "The American" in 1842, and gave the movement the benefit of its columns; and this was the first paper in the State prominently devoted to the cause of the conscience Whigs.

A paper was drawn up by Mr. Wilson, and circulated for signatures, calling a meeting in Boston for consultation and extended effort; and thus was inaugurated the grand movement which ultimately split the Whig party, created the coalition which made Boutwell governor, and sent Charles Sumner to the United-States Senate. There was a deal of work in it, however; and, for the succeeding ten years, Wilson was driving it in all possible ways with never-failing energy, and a faith that wavered not for a moment. The church, the caucus, the county and state conventions of the party, the press, the stump, the House of Representatives, and the Senate, were all turned to account, and marshalled by him to do battle against iniquity. It was all work, this part of it, and work that made no brilliant show; work that could only be done quietly; that would not bear vaunting; for which there were no clapping of hands, banquets, rousing cheers, and applauding criticisms in the daily press: but it was work that saved the reputation of Massachusetts, and work that at last proved the salvation of the country; for, had Massachusetts not kept the banner always flying in the way she did, there would have been no Union to-day, and consequently no peace.

It is not pretended, of course, that other minds in other places were not agitated and earnestly at work to solve the great problem of a nation's freedom. All that is claimed is, that this organization by Wilson and his immediate associates was the one which set in motion the conscience Whig movement; and that movement prevented the entire relapse of the Whig party of the State into the hands of the Lunts, Choates, and Austins, who were allied to the Southern wing of the party, and were engaged in a hot crusade against the antislavery efforts of the time. It was the beginning of the movement that made Massachusetts the head and front of the column of freedom. This might have come in some other way, possibly; but it is the way it did come, and seems to have been a necessary link in the great chain of events which finally overthrew the institution of slavery.

At the commencement of this session (1846), Gov. Briggs laid before the legislature some resolutions concerning slavery and the action of Massachusetts which had been adopted by the legislature of Georgia. Mr. Wilson promptly moved their reference to a special committee, and offered an order that they be instructed to report a preamble and resolution which should express in fitting terms the hostility of Massachusetts to the institution of slavery.

The Whigs and Democrats joined in opposition to this order, but were met by the member from Natick with an argument of great length, and of such force and power that his opponents were glad to tender a compromise in the shape of an amendment, leaving the committee to act without instructions. As the committee were supposed to be all right, and certain to report Mr. Wilson's own views, the compromise was accepted as an easy way to let his opponents down, and save them the mortification of defeat by an open vote on his original motion.

In this speech Wilson took the ground that we must destroy slavery, or slavery will destroy liberty. We must restore our government to its original and pristine purity.

The contest is a glorious one. Let us be cheered by the fact that the bold and daring effort of the slave-power to arrest the progress of free principles has awakened and aroused the nation. That power has won a brilliant victory in the acquisition of Texas; yet it is only one victory in its long series over the constitution and liberties of the country. Other fields are yet to be fought; and if we are true to the country, freedom, and to humanity, the future has yet a Waterloo in store for the supporters of this unholy system. He called upon the party to accept these issues, which were vital; and, if victory came, to hail and improve it; and, if defeat should be their lot, they would still have the glory of having deserved success. For himself, he was ready to act with any man or party — Whig, Democrat, Abolitionist, Christian, or Infidel — who would go for the cause of emancipation.

But Mr. Wilson was too hasty in his judgment as to the probable action of the committee. Having gained the point of leaving them free, efforts were at once put forth to secure a mild and evasive report, which were successful; and he was compelled to make a minority report. In the House, Wilson moved his resolution as a substitute for that of the committee; and it was carried by a vote of a hundred and forty-one to fifty-three, but was lost in the Senate.

The report of the minority was a masterly production, and created a profound sensation in the House and in the State. It set forth, that, by the action of the two houses of Congress, Texas had been blended and indissolubly connected with the republic. Every act in its history, from its first inception to its final consummation, had been a deep disgrace. The fermenting of discord, the levying of troops, the speculation in lands, the dark intrigues which had been plotted, presented a mass of rottenness and corruption. The object of annexation was confessed to be the extension and perpetuation of human bondage. Inspired by that purpose, the South has won one of the most brilliant victories in her long series of victories over the constitution of the country and the liberties of the people. Our Union is not *the* Union our fathers made. That Union has been trampled beneath the iron heel of the triumphant slave-power. We stand on the threshold of a new Union, which the annexation of a foreign nation has created. A new page is opened in the history of the republic. Already the victorious hand of the slave-power points the way to further acquisitions. In this crisis of the country, has Massachusetts nothing to say, nothing to propose, nothing to do? Shall we, indeed, now give up the struggle, confess ourselves vanquished, think all is lost? Shall Massachusetts, now that annexation is accomplished, erase all her solemn protests, shut up as a great mistake the history of a fifty-years' struggle against the influences of slavery, and, by quiet submission and a change of policy, obtain the forgiveness of the slave-power? or shall she yet trust in justice and truth, and, however the lights of other States may waver, stand herself unfaltering on the lofty eminence she has never yet deserted or betrayed, and use free speech, the free press, the free ballot, the freedom of remonstrance, and her other rights and powers, narrow though they be, in such a manner as finally to blot out the greatest disgrace and the most fruitful source of danger which was ever entailed on any nation? The report closed with the declaration that the experience of sixty years afforded ample evidence that only by an adherence far more stern than that of our fathers to the principles of the Declaration of Independence, and a use far more vigorous than theirs of all the powers of self-preservation and defence which the Constitution has secured to the freemen of the Union, will the Union and our liberties be preserved, and with them the hopes of the race for long years to come.

This report of Henry Wilson, his speeches on the main question, and his personal exertions to carry the legislature in favor of the resolves, accomplished the purpose of the people of Natick in returning him to the lower branch of the General Court, gave him the opportunity to display his powers of leadership on a field worthy and every way adapted to his capacity and his wishes, and saved the cause from a further temporary retrocession and defeat. It must be borne in mind that all this was in 1846, or before; that it was all accomplished before Charles Sumner had taken the field as a politician or lecturer, and two years before Horace Mann had opened his powerful batteries upon the advocates of oppression and unrighteousness. Their splendid achievements are not to be depreciated, certainly; but Wilson is an older soldier than either, though younger in years, and was engaged in hot conflict years before they enlisted or took part in the campaign.

The succeeding year, and in 1849, he was returned to the House again, and in 1850 to the Senate, of which body he was chosen president, filling the station with the same ability and success that he did all positions into which he was called.

When President Fillmore visited Massachusetts, Wilson was chairman of the committee of welcome, and made the official address; and performed the same duty when the great Hungarian revolutionist and leader, Kossuth, came to Boston, and received an ovation, that in heartiness, and numbers present, had then never been equalled in the city. The able manner these duties were performed by Wilson was a surprise to many who had looked upon him as a mere political manager, unable to sustain the dignity of the State on occasions of such imposing character.

For the session of 1849 he was the Free-soil candidate for speaker; but, the party being in the minority, he was not elected. During the period we have now passed in this narrative, he was the presiding officer at many conventions of the party; was four years chairman of the State Central Committee, and engineer in general of their principal movements.

CHAPTER V.

As a Politician. — Candidate for Congress. — Whig Convention. — Bolting. — Free Soil. — Coalition. — Election of Sumner.

THE death of John Quincy Adams created a vacancy in the Eighth Congressional District of Massachusetts, in 1848, that no man could expect to fill with equal distinction and to the satisfaction of the people; and yet, on the day before the convention met to make the nomination for his succession, Wilson was ahead of any other candidate. This fact having been pretty well settled, it became apparent to the opponents of Mr. Wilson that he could be prevented from receiving the nomination only by one course; and that was to obtain the consent of Mr. Horace Mann, the Secretary of the Board of Education, to enter the lists against him. Mr. Mann was at the height of his fame as a brilliant orator, statesman, and philanthropist; had long been identified with the institutions which are the glory of Massachusetts; had a national reputation not surpassed by any living man, and a larger personal acquaintance in the district than even John Quincy Adams. He was a native of Norfolk County, which formed the body of the district, but resided then in Newton, the largest of the only five Middlesex towns in the district (Natick being one); and of course had only to signify his willingness to accept a nomination to obtain it. Some gentlemen of Dedham went to see Mr. Mann the night preceding the nomination, and, after long persuasion, obtained his assurance, that, if nominated, he would not decline; and so the nomination was tendered with much unanimity. Wilson's strength was so great, notwithstanding the formidable reputation of his competitor, that he was chosen to represent the district in the National Whig Convention then about to assemble at Philadelphia to nominate

Gen. Taylor for the presidency and to commit suicide, — two purposes it succeeded in accomplishing. Taylor was elected, it is true, but was succeeded by Fillmore, one of those unfortunate New-York politicians who believe that a conglomeration of office-seekers, without any principles in common, can form an administration, and manage national affairs to the satisfaction of everybody. This was attempted: but neither the prestige nor abilities of Daniel Webster and Edward Everett could make it a success; and the party died all the same, as was foreseen by Wilson and Charles Allen. Wilson went to the convention with the clearly-avowed intention of having incorporated in the platform the first fundamental republican principle in a form as strong at least as the Wilmot Proviso, which simply proposed that slavery should not be farther extended. But the convention was unequal to the occasion; nominated Gen. Taylor, who was not known as a Whig, and who was not committed to any Whig principles; and refused to concede any thing to the antislavery sentiment of the party. Wilson and Allen bolted, — not much of a bolt, the Whigs said: only two uninfluential men from down East in fanatical Massachusetts; that was all. The pluck of the men, however, attracted attention; and either would have gone out alone, had the other remained. The pluck, and the principle which they could not sacrifice, saved the act from contempt; and, deep down in many hearts that dared not acknowledge it, there was a profound feeling of respect for these men which mere dickering politicians never arouse when they break away from their party associations.

When Wilson arose and announced his intention not to abide by the action of the convention, there was a wild uproar and howling that would have added to the credit of Bedlam. A delegate from North Carolina secured silence after a while by suggesting that the gentleman was injuring no one but himself: not a remarkably wise observation in view of the fact that Wilson's reputation is world-wide to-day, and that delegate would be unrecognized were his name given.

Wilson came home; wrote an address to his constituents giving an account of proceedings, and explaining and defending his course in withdrawing from the convention. He justified his action on the ground that the resolutions of the convention which nominated him demanded it, and that he could not do otherwise without violating his own professions, and convictions of duty. He closed by saying, " Bitter denunciations have already been heaped upon me; yet I see nothing to retract. No hope of political reward, no fear of ridicule or denunciation, will deter me from acting up to my convictions of duty in resisting the extension of slavery and the arrogant demands of the slave-power."

A few days after Wilson's return home, he was honored by an invitation to meet and confer with the "godlike Daniel" and a few of his particular friends in Boston upon the situation. This was in the olden time; and those were the days when, in and around Boston, there were people who thought Daniel Webster knew a few things concerning politics and kindred topics. If report be true, Mr. Webster was a man, who, with all his virtues and good sense, had not been in the habit of seeking the counsel and advice of the small-potato class of politicians; and he was reputed to have no stomach for humbugs in politics or other things. The sending for Henry Wilson to meet the wise men of the east in conference was certainly an indication that in high quarters our young statesman was not considered altogether a nobody, and that he had attracted the attention of people not much in the habit of looking for objects with a microscope.

The conference was held. Mr. Webster was pleased, made the satirical remark that a "North" had been discovered, and seemed gratified with the opening prospects. But Webster was getting old; and the new country, though discovered, was so far off, and so difficult to reach, that he never emigrated thither, and on the 7th of March, four years later, sold his land-warrant for promises to pay that were worthless, and went to protest at maturity. It is not probable that at this time Mr. Webster contemplated the possibility of Henry Wilson's representing Massachusetts in the United-States Senate for a period as long as his own, and that he would originate and successfully carry through twenty or thirty important measures to his one. He was consulting with a prophet, and didn't know it. The greatest man of his time seeking advice of the shoemaker, rejecting it, and the latter, by following it, reaching the pedestal on which the great man stood! — what a theme for moralists and poets! what a lesson for statesmen and politicians!

The Free-soil party was now formed; Wilson being one of the chief advisers and workers to that end. He was alive with energy, and boiling over with enthusiasm. Conventions, mass-meetings, school-district gatherings, speeches, consultations, and appeals in writing, were the order of the day; and he was everywhere and at all points urging on the glorious cause. The little rill started in Capt. Herring's shop was becoming a mighty river. There was tremendous excitement; and even those old fellows who could not see any cause for it still felt there was something in motion, — an underground swell that was shaking the solid earth, and might end in disaster or a general wreck. Then came the Buffalo Convention, where Wilson was one of the leading spirits, and the nomination of Martin Van Buren and Charles Francis Adams for president and vice-president.

The nomination of Van Buren, who was not a pre-eminent anti-slavery man, was effected very much in the same way that Greeley was nominated at Cincinnati. The convention was captured by the New-York politicians, and fell into such hands that suspicion of its moral purity was excited; and its champions, instead of striking at the enemy all the time, were put on the defensive. "The Tribune" was shocked at the moral degeneracy which could unite with a Democratic faction men like Adams, Sumner, and Wilson, even for the purpose of resisting slavery. It was abominable; it was infamous; it was damnable. Probably no mortal ever suffered such intense pangs at the conduct of others as Greeley did when Giddings, Leavitt, and Palfrey shook hands over the shallow chasm with Dix, Tilden, and Van Buren. What would he have felt had Hendricks, Voorhees, and John Morrisey, been included?

But Gen. Taylor was elected; and, as before remarked, the Whig party, having lost its vital principle, died, or, what is the same thing, became a mere faction, and from that day went out of existence as a political power. The movement with Van Buren was not a success in so far as the election was concerned; but it broke the solidity of the Democratic ranks, and taught some lessons in political engineering to Wilson that were valuable, and which he proposed to apply in the future operations against slavery. In the Democratic party of Massachusetts were a few men of liberal views, progressive ideas, and fine abilities, to whom the iron collars prepared by the Masons and Slidells and Davises of the party for general every-day wear were offensive; prominent among whom were N. P. Banks and George S. Boutwell, two gentlemen, like Wilson, from the ranks, and capable of great things.

The Whigs had lost their temper, and settled down into a state of dogged and sullen perversity. They wanted to die, and were willing to be kicked to death, but not willing to be pushed or persuaded into any course that led to resuscitation or hope. The Free-soil party, not being in the majority, and not being able to dispel the stupidity that had seized upon the Whigs, was in a position to need allies, and not too proud to accept them. Wilson was for moving on the enemy's works, and conceived the idea of working into the United-States Senate a man who would be able from that position to wake up the drowsy nation. He suggested to Banks and Boutwell the feasibility of united operations, to a limited extent, between their two parties. Mr. Banks immediately decided that it would not be possible to make any arrangement, however honest and disinterested, which would not be so misconstrued and misrepresented that it would be defeated. Mr. Boutwell was more cautious, but, on the whole, inclined to the opinion that the experiment could not succeed; or, at any rate, the risks were too dangerous. But Wilson was aware that the idea was new to them; and resolved, after they had pondered it a few days, to broach the subject again. In a little time he found the plan was gaining in favor; and, by careful and judicious pressing, it shortly began to take with the leading men of both the Free-soil and Democratic parties, and finally developed into what was termed the "coalition," and became successful.

The plan was a very simple one: merely to run separate candidates for governor, and unite on members of the legislature in towns where the two parties, by combining, could elect their men. As it required a majority vote to elect the governor, there would be no choice by the people, and the legislature would make the governor. It was understood from the start that the Free-soil party wanted the United-States senator, and would unite for nothing less; and it was understood that they wanted Charles Sumner. In order to carry out such an arrangement, it was of the first importance that good men should be selected as candidates. The Democrats found in George S. Boutwell the man for the occasion. He was very young to stand as a candidate for gubernatorial honors in the ancient Commonwealth where years were thought essential to such a dignified station; but he was an intrepid debater who had won laurels in the House, a cool calculator, free from all nonsense, a man of the people, and without damaging affiliations. He was nominated, and received the support of his party; but there was no choice, and so he went to the legislature as one of the constitutional candidates, where, by aid of the Free-soil members, he was elected governor. Wilson was chosen president of the Senate; and Banks, speaker of the House: but this was not contemplated in the original arrangement, and was not a thing that could have been considered until after the legislature had been elected.

The Free-soil folks having performed their part of the stipulation, and elected Boutwell governor, now nominated Charles Sumner for senator, and presented him for the suffrages of the Democratic members of the legislature. To those who are unacquainted with the kinds and quantities of medicines the doctors of the old school were in the habit of prescribing for their patients, this would naturally be regarded as about the heaviest dose a not very sick party could be called upon to swallow. It wouldn't be any thing now: there are indications that it might be agreeable to the Democracy to take a small dose of Sumner. But Democracy in 1851 was not the sick man it is to-day: it was strong and robust, and, as a national organization, under control of the slave-power. Its great horror was abolitionism; and Charles Sumner was, in its esteem, about the most virulent sample of that vile drug that could be produced. The Democrats had secured their governor; and here was a fine opportunity to hedge, to put country above party, to rise above paltry bargains, and perhaps save the Union, — a thing very much in the Democratic line at that period. Having been paid in advance, it could be done without loss; and so, when they came to ballot for the senator, the coalition which had been strong enough to elect Boutwell was found not quite strong enough to elect Sumner.

And so they balloted and balloted, and then consulted and balloted, and balloted and consulted: and days went by, and there was no choice; and weeks went by, and still no choice; and Charles Sumner was not yet a United-States senator. Will he ever be? That was a great question. For the future fame of Sumner it was *the* great question; and a momentous one it was. Two things were requisite at this immensely critical time, — indomitable perseverance in the leadership, and absolute integrity in the leaders, of the Free-soil party. The leader of the party was the president of the Senate, the originator of the coalition, — Henry Wilson. The scheme of the Democrats who did not vote for Sumner was, to dictate the man whom they would vote for; and he, owing thus his election to them, would find a hook in his nose by which the schemers could control him. It was a dangerous moment; and the scheme had been concocted by that craftiest of manipulators, Caleb Cushing, who was a member of the House, and never idle, especially when any profound games were waiting to be played. There were various devices suggested and canvassed; but the only one which concerns this biography is that which included Wilson as the prime figure. When they had become weary with repeated voting, and there were hints among the Free-soil men that the case was hopeless, and Sumner was out of the question, the Democrats, who had scattered, sent one of their number to Wilson with the offer, that if Sumner could be withdrawn, and Wilson substituted, there should be an election on the next ballot. The offer was not taken; and then Caleb came in person, and gave his personal guaranty that the snarl should be unravelled at once if Wilson would but stand in Sumner's shoes as the senatorial candidate.

But Wilson could not be moved. A seat in the Senate was within his grasp: he had but to say the word, and take it. He declined, and insisted that not a man should think for one moment of voting for any one but Sumner: to do otherwise would demoralize the coalition, and turn it into a jobbing concern for the benefit of individuals. Charles Sumner was the nominee. The coalition was not formed for his personal benefit, nor for George S. Boutwell's: it was formed to give Massachusetts a State government not under the control of powerful corporations, and a senator who could wake up the echoes of freedom in the Capitol of the nation; and they must keep voting till doomsday, if need be, to accomplish this result.

The firmness of Wilson saved the day: and, when it was found impossible to move him, one Democrat changed; and, on the twenty-sixth ballot, Charles Sumner was elected.

When the deed was done, people saw how it was done, and how it only could have been done. No one doubted that Wilson elected Sumner; and Mr. Sumner wrote him a letter of thanks, in which he acknowledged, that but for his foresight, consummate skill, and unexampled pertinacity, the election could not have been effected. Charles Sumner, therefore, as a senatorial gift to the nation, was a present from Henry Wilson; and the Democratic fuglemen who now have such a high appreciation of the value of the gift have a grand opportunity to reward the giver by assisting him to a new position of honor and usefulness.

This was the most memorable contest for the senatorship that any State in the Union ever witnessed, whether we take into consideration the state of parties and their relations to each other, the long severity of the contest, the even balance of the ballotings, or the tremendous results that have ensued. The hopes of Wilson were realized in full. Sumner in the Senate was the right man in the right place. He bombarded the old hulk of slavery with a vigor that told, and damaged it beyond recovery. Sumner had his opportunity, and improved it for his own benefit and for the benefit of the nation; and he may live to see the day when he will be glad to acknowledge, that, in parting company from the man who first set him up in business, he made the grandest mistake of his whole life.

CHAPTER VI.

Constitutional Convention. — Elected by Two Towns. — Leadership. — Debates. — Chosen President *pro tem.*

THE convention to revise the Constitution of Massachusetts met in Boston May 4, 1853, and made choice of N. P. Banks, jun., for its presiding officer. It was composed of men of eminent ability from all the leading professions and occupations of life. Men like Jacob Bigelow, Luther V Bell, and Foster Hooper, of the medical profession; George Putnam, Dr. Blagden, Dr. Braman, Dr. Lothrop, and C. W. Upham, of the clergy; and nearly all the lawyers of distinction in the State, — were among the members. Rufus Choate, Sidney Bartlett, B. F. Hallett, B. F. Butler, Peleg Sprague, Marcus Morton, Joel Parker, Otis P. Lord, Simon Greenleaf, Charles Sumner, George S. Hillard, R. H. Dana, and hosts of others, judges, professors, district attorneys, and practitioners, were there, constituting a galaxy of names that could hardly be matched by any bar in the country. Sprague had been a distinguished member of the United-States Senate in the palmy days of Clay, Calhoun, Webster, Silas Wright, and Tom Benton; Choate had been United-States senator, was now attorney-general, and at the height of his fame; while others had been chief justices of States, governors, and candidates of their parties for many years. The ablest merchants and business-men were also there in force, — George B. Upton, George S. Boutwell, James Read, J. T. Stevenson, James M. Beebe, and others; with political orators of brilliancy like Edward L. Keyes, Anson Burlingame, H. L. Dawes, Charles Allen, N. P. Banks, and many too numerous to mention.

In a convention of such men, no man of inferior abilities would be able to stand a single moment in a leading position; but Henry Wilson, the mechanic, the "cobbler" if you will, was not only a member, but was accorded the position to which, as a representative man and an organizing power, he was entitled.

He was made chairman of the committee to provide the order of business, with Choate, Dawes, Cushman, Beach, Nayson, Hale, and Aspinwall for colleagues. The splendid parliamentary abilities of N. P. Banks, another mechanic, secured for him the presidency of the convention; and its next highest and equally-important position was taken by Wilson, — a position analogous to the chairmanship of Ways and Means in the House. There was one peculiarity attending the election of Wilson to the convention. He had been chosen by two towns, Natick and Berlin; and the circumstances were these: He had been one of the originators of the convention; was in favor of certain reforms that were desired by the majority of the people; and his talents and information were needed in the body. But Natick politically was then so nearly equally divided, that his election was not to be counted upon as certain. To make sure of his being there, the people of Berlin consented to adopt him, they having the power to elect any one, and he being highly esteemed and respected there. He therefore accepted their offer of a seat, and declined the suffrages of his own townsmen. The night before the election, however, it came to the comprehension of the people of Natick, that, in so distinguished a body as would soon assemble, the honor of being represented by a man who must necessarily be a cipher therein was not to be coveted; and, rallying, Wilson was triumphantly nominated in lieu of the other man, and the next day elected, proving that two stools do not necessarily involve a lodgement, to be avoided by the party who mounts them. Wilson went over to Berlin, called the people together, explained to their satisfaction, and obtained a unanimous release of his obligation to serve them; they accepting Gov. Boutwell, who had failed of an election in his own town of Groton. But, at the opening of the convention, Berlin was not represented, the vacancy made by the declination of Wilson not having been filled yet; and one of the longest and ablest debates of the session grew out of this particular case, in which was involved the question of the powers of the legislature and the sovereignty of the people.

This debate commenced May 6, and lasted till May 18, during a portion of the sittings; and was participated in by Hallett, Train, Parker, Allen, Choate, Wilson, and other leading speakers.

The points to-day are not agitated, and there is no need to explain them; but the conclusion of Wilson's speech in reply to Choate will show the different ideas of the two men, and the classes they represented.

Mr. Wilson. — "I do not, Mr. President, regret the time consumed by this debate. It has been conducted with eminent ability; and I am quite sure we have more distinct views of the questions so fully and ably discussed that will not be lost to us. Opinions have been advanced by gentlemen, which, in my judgment, are at war with the whole doctrine of popular sovereignty as defined in our constitutions, pronounced by our judicial tribunals, understood by our statesmen, and practised by our people, since the sovereign power passed from England to the American people. The real, actual, living sovereignty of the people is not yet comprehended by some men of learning and talent. They regard it, as Mr. Calhoun regarded the Declaration of Independence, as a 'rhetorical flourish.' Our history is marked by what Mr. Madison calls the 'little, ill-timed scruples' of men who indulge, under the mask of zeal for adhering to ordinary forms, their secret animosity to the substance contended for.

"Mr. President, the gentleman from Boston (Mr. Choate), in his brilliant speech the other day, which so delighted us all, implored us to 'spare the rust of the Constitution.' I had thought, sir, that our free democratic institutions were to be ever new, bright, perennial. I had thought that these institutions were to be ever renewed by the popular intelligence; made to conform to the ever-advancing spirit of the ages, and the wants of the living people. I had thought that the marked feature of our institutions was, that they were ever to be kept free from the 'rust of ages,' and to be imbued with the living, actual life of the people. I would not allow rust to gather upon our constitution of government, but would keep it as bright as when it came from the hands of the statesmen who framed it, and of the people who breathed into it vitality and force." Choate was not fond of glittering things, except his own speeches; and Wilson was for polishing up occasionally.

On the 19th of May, Wilson presented the report of the committee in favor of making single senatorial districts on the basis of population; taking the ground distinctly that there was no reason why Lowell should be cut down in the basis because of its ten thousand women, or Boston because of its fifty thousand Irishmen and Germans. "Upon political questions there may be differences of opinion; but upon nineteen-twentieths of the questions that come before the legislature, your women, your foreign population, and your persons who cannot vote, have a deep and abiding personal interest." And again, same debate: "I am not one of those who expect to advocate the right of women to vote. But one thing is certain: I could not make an argument against it; and I would like to see the man who could make such an argument. And I go farther: I believe, that, upon most of the questions that concern this commonwealth and this country, they have their influence; and if they had also the right to vote, the country would be none the worse governed. The foreign population is engaged in the business-affairs of life, — in our churches and our schools, in the various pursuits of social life, and in every thing that is consistent with the duties of citizens; and they influence the opinions of their neighbors and friends. Sir, the honorable representative on this floor from Boston, if he be worthy of the seat he fills, will pay deference to the sentiments of that portion of the community who cannot vote, as well as that portion who can." These sentiments were uttered nineteen years ago.

On the 27th of May Mr. Wilson made a strong speech against changing elections from the majority system to a plurality, asserting that reforms spring from the bosom of the people, who are often checkmated by caucuses and combinations of politicians; and the plurality system aids the latter by forcing upon the voters a choice of evils. He declared that many of the evils of popular government in the several States were directly traceable to the plurality system of elections.

On the 28th he spoke again on the question of making aliens ineligible to the office of governor, and said, "I see no necessity of putting these words, 'citizens of the United States,' into the Constitution. I am content that a citizen of Massachusetts shall be governor of Massachusetts if the people choose to make him so. According to my understanding of the Constitution, a man who is not a naturalized citizen of the State or the Union could be elected governor of this Commonwealth to-day. . . . I care nothing about the place where a man was born: I do not wish to bring the question into this discussion, and I do not like to have such words as 'foreign birth' incorporated in the Constitution."

On the 30th May he spoke against high-sounding titles for State offices, and against a proposition to make the lieutenant-governor the presiding officer of the Senate.

On the 7th of June Mr. Wilson distinguished himself by a long and very able argument in favor of the secret ballot, which would enable the poor man to vote without being under fear of losing employment in consequence of voting contrary to the wishes of the rich and domineering manufacturer. He quoted the opinions of Grote, Macaulay, Cobden, Bright, O'Connell, and other liberal and reform statesmen in Europe, in favor of the scheme, and of the Duke of Wellington, Sir James Graham, and Sir Robert Peel, of the Tories, against it. Referring to the latter, he said, "Sir, we have a class of men in this country who have just such opinions. They always discover we are going to ruin. We have been marching on for sixty years in a course of progress unexampled in the history of the world; and all that time these men have thought that the country was finished and 'fenced in,' and that all progress tended to ruin. Massachusetts has had, and now has, her full share of these timid creatures, who have little confidence in, or knowledge of, the people. If these men would mingle more with the masses, they would imbibe something of that spirit of hope and confidence which animates the people in their onward march in the career of democratic progress and reform. . . . I trust this convention will put into the Constitution of Massachusetts this fundamental principle; and I trust they will also put into the Constitution the *vivâ-voce* mode of voting for the legislators; and that while we have secured to the people the right to vote, with no eye upon them but the eye of God, free from dictation and intimidation from any quarter, we shall force the representatives to vote in the broad and open light of day."

On the 11th of June he was on the floor advocating the abolition of the poll-tax as a qualification for voting. He said, "Men should, and they will, pay their poll-taxes, if they are able to do so; but, if they are not able to, they should not have their rights denied them because they are poor. If a man does not pay his tax, you have the power to arrest him and to imprison him. If he has the means to pay, he will, rather than go to jail; but if he is poor, if he cannot pay his tax, he ought not to be compelled, or forfeit his rights. Poverty is bitter enough to be borne without disfranchisement. The man of toil who has reared a family, contributed hundreds of dollars by indirect taxation to support the government, who may perhaps have given his blood to the defence of the country, who has paid his taxes cheerfully for years, should not, as life begins to cast its shadows over him, as his arm begins to fail and his step to totter, be degraded because he, in his old age, is compelled to drink the cup of poverty. That constitutional provision which would deny to the poor man who could not pay his tax the right to vote should be forever blotted out of the constitution of a Christian commonwealth. Another reason for its adoption is this: Suffrage is a right which should be sacredly guarded. No man should hold this right subject to the mistakes of a board of assessors." It would appear that he was at his post every day, watching jealously all the propositions calculated to curtail the rights of the working-man and the poor, ready at all times to enter upon the defence of the humble, knowing exactly where every measure infringes on the interests of those who have no money and no influence, and able to point out the faults of systems that have kept men out of their rights, and denied them the privileges that would enable them to rise.

On the 20th, 21st, and 22d of June, the militia was under discussion; and, as the rights of colored men to serve as soldiers or become members of the independent military organizations were to be determined by the action of the convention, Wilson felt called upon to face the then existing strong prejudice against the colored race, which, till now, effectually excluded them; and accordingly threw himself into the debate with great zeal on their behalf, speaking several times with earnestness and his usual ability. He proposed an amendment to the provision reported by the committee in these words: "*Resolved*, That no distinction shall ever be made in the organization of the volunteer militia of this Commonwealth on account of color or race." This proposition, so universally popular now, and conceded by even the great Democratic party to be out of the contest, was then thought fanatical and dangerous to the last degree, and was opposed by the most liberal Democrats, and assailed as being in violation of the spirit and letter of the laws and constitution of the United States. Another strong objection to the amendment in the minds of many was, that it would not only admit colored men into the militia, but unnaturalized foreigners; but Wilson claimed this right for all, irrespective of race or color. The tone of these speeches is indicated by the following extract: "The first victim of the Boston massacre on the 5th of March, 1770, which made the fires of resistance burn more intensely, was a colored man. Hundreds of colored men entered the ranks, and fought bravely in the Revolution. Graydon in his Memoirs informs us that many Southern officers disliked the New-England regiments because so many colored men were in their ranks. At Red Bank they received the commendation of the commander for gallant conduct.

"A colored battalion was organized for the defence of New Orleans; and Gen. Jackson publicly thanked them for courage and conduct. When the country has required their blood in days of conflict and trial, they have given it freely, and we have accepted; but in times of peace, when their blood is not needed, we spurn and trample them under foot. I have no part in this great wrong to a race. Wherever and whenever we have the power to do it, I would give to all men of every clime and race, of every creed and faith, freedom and equality before the law. My voice and my vote shall ever be given for the equality of all the children of men before the laws of the Commonwealth of Massachusetts and the United States."

The difference between Mr. Wilson, and the Whigs represented by Choate, and the Democrats represented by Mr. Hallett, was expressed by the latter, when he declared, that although the Massachusetts Constitution made no distinction on account of color, and made the governor commander-in-chief of the militia, should the people elect a colored man governor he could not take command of the militia, because, by the laws of Congress, he would not be eligible to office in the militia, or be connected with it.

June 28, Mr. Wilson spoke against the proposal to prohibit

the loaning of the credit of the State for public improvements, taking the ground that past experience had fully justified the policy, and that the people could be trusted to exercise the power judiciously. He remarked, "I do not think wisdom will die out with this convention. I look upon this convention as a very able body of men; but there will be wiser men to come here twenty years hence. I hope, twenty years hence, another convention will sit here; for, whatever may be the result of this convention, in my judgment the expense attending it will be more than repaid by the fact that for two years the people of the State have been discussing fundamental principles, and examining those great principles that underlie our Constitution, and that are embodied in our fundamental laws."

July 6, there was a little *brush* between Mr. Hillard of Boston and the member from Natick. Sharp language was used by both these gentlemen, for which they mutually apologized; and no permanent ill-will was maintained by either. Wilson said it was the first time in eight years' service in deliberative bodies that he had allowed offensive personalities to escape him, and he disclaimed all malice and evil intent in the present instance.

July 19, Wilson spoke earnestly in favor of an order limiting the pay of the members to days of actual attendance unless they were detained at home by sickness, and gave some valuable statistics relating to the non-attendance of members of the House of Representatives.

On the opening of the convention, July 21, information came that Hon. N. P. Banks, its president, was detained at home by sickness: whereupon the record shows the following action:—

"Mr. Rantoul of Beverly moved that the convention proceed to the election of a president *pro tempore* by nomination.

"The motion was agreed to.

"Mr. Rantoul nominated Henry Wilson of Natick, and moved that he be president *pro tempore* of the convention.

"The motion was unanimously agreed to.

"The secretary appointed Messrs. Briggs of Pittsfield, and Boutwell for Berlin, to conduct Mr. Wilson to the chair."

George N. Briggs and George S. Boutwell were two ex-governors of the State; and hence their selection to do the honors of the occasion. Those persons who are troubled about the qualifications of Mr. Wilson to preside over the Senate may see in this action of the Massachusetts Constitutional Convention, which had among its members Briggs, Boutwell, Butler, Dawes, Choate, Sumner, and Dana, an indorsement that should be sufficiently convincing so far as authority can go, and one that few men could hope to obtain. Many of the most important orders and amendments adopted by the convention were framed, introduced, and engineered by Henry Wilson; and its work, as finally completed, was more the result of his energetic labor and thought than that of any single mind.

It failed before the people in consequence of not meeting the views of the Irish voters in an important respect; but for this Wilson was not responsible: but most of the amendments proposed have since been incorporated into the Constitution by legislative action and the direct vote of the people.

The speeches of Mr. Wilson in this convention are all characterized by strong common sense, liberal views, devotion to popular rights, force of statement, and manly, vigorous eloquence. They were crowded with facts, and will ever remain a solid and positive contribution to the cause of constitutional and legislative reform.

CHAPTER VII.

The American Movement.

THE Massachusetts Constitutional Convention of 1853 incorporated a provision forbidding the appropriation of public money for the support of sectarian schools. This was unquestionably the cause of the defeat of the Constitution before the people; a large portion of the Irish Catholic vote being thrown against the Constitution, it was alleged, on account of this provision. This action created some feeling in the State, and probably contributed somewhat to the rapid growth of the American organizations which sprang up in the spring and summer of 1854.

The proposition of Mr. Douglas to repeal so much of the Missouri Compromise as prohibited slavery west of the Mississippi, and north of 36° 30′, agitated Congress, and profoundly stirred the popular mind. The aggressive policy of the South, the servility of Northern politicians, and especially the conduct of the Southern Whigs, alarmed the people, and begat a strong desire on the part of many for a union of effort, among the friends of freedom and of the country, against these encroachments. While the Kansas-Nebraska Bill was pending in Congress, Mr. Wilson took part in the canvass in New Hampshire. On his return to Massachusetts, he prepared and delivered a speech in several places in opposition to this repeal, and in favor of the union of all its opponents. It was printed, and received the warm commendations of Mr. Seward, Mr. Chase, and Mr. Sumner. Hoping to do something to bring about this union, Mr. Wilson went to Washington, was present when the measure passed the House, consulted with Dr. Bailey and many of the leading members of both Houses of Congress, and returned to Massachusetts inspired with the hope that a great party would soon be formed on the basis of freedom, that would render effective the opposition of the people to these fearful and endangering aggressions.

On the 31st of May, a State convention of the Free-soil party was held in Boston. Theophilus P. Chandler presided; and a series of resolutions especially denunciatory of the Fugitive-slave Law and the Kansas-Nebraska Act were passed. Eloquent addresses were made by Amasa Walker, John Pierpont, John A. Andrew, Joshua R. Giddings, and John P. Hale. The resolutions and speeches alike breathed the spirit of unity and a desire for the union of the people in behalf of imperilled liberty.

Mr. Wilson addressed the convention. After referring to the principles, measures, and policy of the free Democracy, he said, "While we adhere to these principles, we say to the members of all parties that we are ready to act with them. If there is a 'forlorn hope' to be led, we will lead it; and others may take and wear the honors. But we go with none who do not wear our principles upon their foreheads, and have them engraved upon their hearts." He maintained that the first duty of the freemen of the North was the extermination of the forty traitors who had voted for the Kansas-Nebraska Act, and to elect a hundred and fifty-eight Northern representatives in favor of its repeal, and for the repeal also of the infamous Fugitive-slave Act. "Let us," he said, "yield up our organizations, every thing but our principles, to establish the great party of the North. The time has now come to forget the past, obliterate the Fugitive-slave Act as well as the Nebraska Act, and to do what we can to place the country perpetually on the side of freedom. The time has now come for the freemen of the North to form one great progressive Democratic party that shall guide the policy and control the destinies of the republic. Whether the standard-bearer of that party shall be our own trusted leader of 1852, or a member of the Whig or Democratic party, he shall have the unwavering support of the free Democracy." These sentiments were warmly and enthusiastically applauded.

During the next few weeks several conferences were held in Boston between leading Free-soilers and a few members of the Whig and Democratic parties in favor of uniting the opponents of the repeal of the Missouri prohibition, and of forming a political organization that should be untrammelled by slaveholding alliances. But the leading men and presses of these parties discouraged the movement; and but few Whigs or Democrats took part in it. In spite, however, of these discouragements, papers were circulated calling a mass convention of the people, to be held at Worcester on the 20th of July.

When the convention assembled, it was found that but few of the dominant party were present. Free-soilers, who had labored for months to unite the opponents of the Kansas-Nebraska measure, saw, as clearly as did their enemies, that the attempted fusion was a failure, and that it had little support from either the Whig or Democratic party. Leading Whig presses characterized it as "a mere Free-soil movement," a "trap" for the Whigs, and pronounced it, as it was, "a failure." Undiscouraged by this opposition to the attempted fusion of parties, the convention declared in favor of a new organization, to be called the "Republican" party; and earnest speeches were made in its behalf. Mr. Wilson took strong ground in favor of the fusion of parties on anti-slavery principles, preferring fusion, he said, to a coalition. "We are assembled to-day," he said, "to forget the differences engendered by past conflicts, and to unite for the overthrow of the slave-holding oligarchy. The Free-soilers will follow where the banner on which their principles are inscribed shall lead. If coalitions had been necessary to advance the cause of freedom by the election of Hale, Sumner, and Chase, to the Senate of the United States, I am ready for a coalition. But a union of men who agree in principle is far better. If we cannot have union, however, give us some arrangement which will advance those principles, and place champions of those principles on the floor of Congress to battle for them."

A State convention of the Republican party was held at Worcester on the 7th of September. But few members who had acted with the Whig and Democratic parties were present. It was composed mainly of Free-soilers. Mr. Wilson was nominated as candidate for governor; and Mr. Increase Sumner of Berkshire County was nominated for lieutenant-governor. Though it was evident the fusion had signally failed, and that the vote would be a small one, Mr. Wilson accepted the nomination. The ticket received little support from persons who had acted with the Whig party, and none from the Whig press. The Whigs maintained intact their organization; and their convention, which met soon afterward, adhered to their national organization, and still appealed for support to the people, though they had been so sadly betrayed by their Southern allies.

It became every day more apparent that the attempt to unite the opponents of the repeal of the Missouri prohibition into one party had signally failed in Massachusetts. But Mr. Wilson was among those who believed that every thing else should be subordinated to the success of the antislavery cause, and that, to advance that cause in Massachusetts, the dominant parties who still adhered to their Southern alliances should be defeated. After consulting with other leading Free-soilers, he, with several others, resolved to co-operate with a secret organization that had existed for a few months, and was increasing in numbers with great rapidity. When the convention of that organization assembled in October, it was strong in numbers, though none anticipated the wonderful victory achieved that year. The Free-soilers and Democrats that had sent Mr. Sumner and Mr. Rantoul to the United-States Senate, and made Mr. Boutwell governor, were in the majority. After the organization of the convention, a motion was made to proceed to the nomination for governor. Mr. Wilson's name was proposed, and received with enthusiastic applause. Mr. Wilson then rose amid great excitement, and said, in substance, that he had arisen to withdraw peremptorily his name as a candidate. He had been nominated by the Republican party, just organized, for governor; had accepted that nomination, and should support the ticket nominated at Worcester; and could not therefore, in honor, accept a nomination, if tendered, by the convention. Principle and sound policy alike forbade. For years he had labored to bring into being a party of freedom. Since the passage of the Kansas-Nebraska Act, he and other antislavery men had striven to unite the people of Massachusetts in such a party. He and they had repeatedly avowed their readiness to sacrifice names, organizations, themselves, every thing but the sacred cause, to unite the people in resistance to the slave-power; but their efforts had signally failed. He had come to the convention in the hope that something would be done to break up the Whig and Democratic parties of Massachusetts, and elect a senator and representatives to Congress with no Southern alliances. To accomplish such results he was ready to make any personal sacrifice, and so was the great body of the antislavery men of the State. Sound policy required that the nominees of that convention for governor and lieutenant-governor should be taken from the Whig and Democratic parties; and he appealed to his personal and political friends to cast no votes for him.

Mr. Wilson gave his vote to the Republican State ticket nominated at Worcester, but used his influence to elect a legislature and a delegation in Congress who would be true to the policy of freedom.

Seven Free-soilers were sent to Congress, and with them N. P. Banks, who had been a coalition Democrat; James Buffinton, who had favored Mr. Sumner's election to the Senate; Linus B. Comins, who had refused in 1848 to vote for Gen. Taylor; and Robert B. Hall, one of the original twelve members of the New-England Antislavery Society. A legislature was elected which Theodore Parker declared to be the strongest antislavery legislative body that had ever assembled in Massachusetts. It passed an act to protect personal liberty, an act against excluding from public schools children on account of race or color, and adopted an address to the governor in favor of removing Judge Loring on account of his agency in returning to slavery Anthony Burns.

Not less than twenty thousand of the twenty-seven thousand Free-soil voters in the State went into the American organization; thus indorsing Mr. Wilson, and securing a preponderating influence in favor of liberty.

The results of the election were no less a surprise to Mr. Wilson, Mr. Burlingame, and other antislavery men who had acted in or co-operated with the American party, than to the people of the State. But the victory threw upon antislavery men the gravest responsibilities. It was clearly their duty to use the influence and power it gave them for the advancement of the cause to which they were pledged by acts, declared opinions, and years of earnest and persistent effort. Though the work involved grave difficulties, they entered upon it with unflagging zeal and unfaltering resolution.

When the legislature assembled, it was found that a large majority of the House were in favor of sending Mr. Wilson to the Senate of the United States. To him this was a surprise; for he had felt, and had said to his friends, after his declination of the nomination made by the American Convention, that personally he had nothing to gain by the election. Before the meeting of the legislature, he had visited no member, spent no money, nor had he asked any one to vote for him. But the antislavery men were in a majority in the legislature, and he received a hundred and four majority in the House, and one majority in the Senate; though, had a second vote been called for, it was known that he would have received twenty-seven votes from the forty members of the latter body.

When Mr. Wilson arrived at Washington, he saw, at a glance, that Southern politicians who had deserted their Northern associates upon the repeal of the Missouri Compromise were striving to impose upon the American organization the test of fidelity to the slave-power. Flattering words from veteran statesmen were poured into his ears. "Flattering appeals," he said in a speech at Springfield, "were made to me to aid in the work of nationalizing the party; but I resolved that upon my soul the sin and shame of silence or submission should never rest. I returned home, determined to baffle, if I could, the meditated treason to freedom and to the North." During five months succeeding the adjournment of Congress, he visited thirteen States, travelled more than nine thousand miles, addressed tens of thousands of freemen, consulted with many leading men, and wrote hundreds of letters. In his speeches and letters he warned antislavery men against the purposes of proslavery leaders North and South, and appealed to antislavery men of all parties to unite in one great political organization, based upon a full recognition of the equal rights of men of every color and race. In an address upon the condition of the antislavery cause, delivered at the Tabernacle in the city of New York, he said, "If my voice could be heard by the antislavery men of all parties, I would say to them, 'Resolve it, write it over your door-posts, engrave it on the lids of your Bibles, proclaim it at the rising of the sun and at the going-down of the same, and in the broad light of noon, that the day any party — be it Whig, Democratic, or American — raises its finger to arrest the antislavery movement, to repress antislavery sentiments, or proscribe antislavery men, it shall surely begin to die.'"

On the 26th of May, 1855, Mr. Wilson addressed the citizens of Brattleborough, Vt., on "The Position and Duty of the American Party." In this speech he declared it to be "the first duty of a public man to see to it that he and those with whom he acted were right in their principles and policies, aims and end." "The hour has now come," he said, "which is to decide whether the American movement is to be a liberal, progressive movement, American in spirit, principle, and policy; or whether it shall be narrow and intolerant, anti-American in spirit, principle, and policy. If I comprehend it at all, — its genius and spirit, its objects and purposes, — it simply proposes to correct and reform abuses and corruptions, to modify and improve the naturalization laws, and to create a public sentiment that shall tend to make the distinct races and nationalities in America one homogeneous people, — Americans all in sentiment and feeling."

"He had," he said, "no sympathy with that narrow, bigoted, intolerant spirit that would make war upon a race of men because they happened to be born in other lands, — a dastardly spirit, that would repel from our shores the men who sought homes here under our free institutions. Such a spirit was anti-American, devilish: he loathed it from the bottom of his heart.

"He knew there were men who called themselves Americans who would abolish the naturalization laws altogether; who would forever deny the right of suffrage to men for the fault of being born out of America. He had no sympathy, and he hoped the men of Vermont had no sympathy, with that class of men whose opinions were at war with the spirit of American institutions and the laws of humanity. Such anti-American sentiments had brought dishonor upon the American movement; and, unless they received the rebuke of the American party, they would defeat the real reforms contemplated, and cover the movement with dishonor.

"He regretted to say that there were some members of the American party in favor of excluding by constitutional amendments all adopted citizens from office. He deeply deplored the action of the legislature of Massachusetts in proposing an amendment to the Constitution embodying this doctrine. He hoped the gentlemen who had given their votes for this proposition — a proposition that would not permit Prof. Agassiz, one of the first living scientific men of the age, to fill, under State appointment, an office even of a scientific character — would see their error, and retreat at once from a position justice, reason, and religion condemned. What little influence he possessed would be given with a hearty good-will to defeat that proposition. He had no sympathy whatever with the spirit that would send out of the country the sons and daughters of misfortune, who, by the storms of life, were thrown upon us for support. Whenever the authorities of the Old World sent their poor here to be relieved themselves of their support, he would promptly redress the imposition: such an abuse ought to be immediately corrected. But when a poor man lands upon our soil, and, by the misfortunes of life, is thrown upon the public charity for support, he would as soon send a poor, fleeing bondman back to the land

> 'Where the cant of democracy dwells on the lips
> Of the forgers of fetters, and wielders of whips,'

as to banish such a man from the land he has sought. There is a kind of native Americanism far more alien to America than are the adopted sons of the Old World it would degrade into servile races. True, genuine Americanism rebukes bigotry, intolerance, and proscription; reforms abuses; adopts a wise, humane, and Christian policy towards all men, — a policy consistent with the idea that 'all men are created equal.'

"If the American party is to achieve any thing for good, it must adopt a wise and humane policy consistent with our democratic ideas, — a policy which will reform existing abuses, and guard against future ones: which shall combine in one harmonious organization moderate and patriotic men who love freedom and hate oppression.

"Upon the grand and overshadowing question of American slavery the American party must take its position. If it wishes a speedy death and a dishonored grave, let it adopt the policy of neutrality upon that question, or the policy of ignoring that question. If that party wishes to live, to impress its policy upon the nation, it must repudiate the sectional policy of slavery, and stand upon the broad and national basis of freedom. It must boldly accept the position that 'freedom is national, and slavery is sectional.' It must stand upon the national idea embodied in the Declaration of Independence, that 'all men are created equal, and have an inalienable right to life, liberty, and the pursuit of happiness.' It must accept these words as embracing the great central, national idea of America, fidelity to which is national in New England and in South Carolina. It must recognize the doctrine, that the Constitution of the United States was made 'TO SECURE THE BLESSINGS OF LIBERTY;' that Congress has no right to make a slave, or allow slavery to exist outside of the slave States; and that the Federal Government must be relieved from all connection with and responsibility for slavery."

Referring to the brilliant victories that had been achieved in New England, the Great West, Pennsylvania, and New Jersey, by the union of antislavery men, Whigs, and anti-Nebraska Democrats, he spoke in condemnation of those, especially in New York, who maintained that Americans should occupy a neutral position on the slavery question; and he expressed his gratification at their defeat.

These views brought upon Mr. Wilson sharp criticisms and bitter denunciations. This feeling was specially manifested in the National Council, which assembled in Philadelphia early in June. The men who were striving to make the American party proslavery, proscriptive, and intolerant, denounced him as an abolitionist and a disorganizer. During several days, the council was convulsed, rent, and torn by the issues touching slavery.

The leadership of the antislavery men was, by common consent of friend and foe, accorded to Mr. Wilson. "Gen. Wilson was," said "The Springfield Republican," "not only the leading delegate of Massachusetts, but of the free States, at the late Philadelphia National Council. No man exercised so great an influence in that body. He was the master-spirit of the North; and but for his energy and industry, moderation in demand, and firmness in maintenance, combined with his parliamentary ability on the floor of the council, the result on the part of the free States must have been less creditable to themselves and their delegates.

"It is but simple justice to say that he was the hero of the contest. This merit, we believe, will be awarded to him by the delegates of both the North and South, who felt the force of his labors either for or against their convictions. It is true, Gen. Wilson did no more than his duty, considering his position and the State he represented. But this could have been truly said had he done less. Duty is relative, and not always measurable; and where so many were weak and faithless, where defection was rife, and treason not wanting, he who gave his whole energy, his whole thought, and almost his whole time, sacrificing rest, and even sleep, to encouraging the timid, convincing the doubtful, stiffening the faltering, and marshalling all up to the true expectation of the North, at the same time that he defied the personal and political assaults of hot-headed Southerners, and with earnest eloquence proudly spoke the purposes and pretensions of freedom, and warred with resistless denunciation and sarcasm the ranks of the doughfaces, — even if this were only duty, it is a performance of duty worthy of distinguished credit and high encomium. He received it there from all his associates, while he challenged the admiration and respect of the generous and high-minded of those who opposed his conclusions and resisted his energetic assaults."

The committee, by a vote of seventeen to fourteen, reported in favor of abiding by and maintaining the existing laws upon the subject of slavery as a final and conclusive settlement. It reported against any legislation prohibiting slavery in the Territories, or abolishing it in the District of Columbia.

Mr. Wilson took the lead in resistance to the adoption of that illiberal, proslavery, and intolerant platform. "The adoption of the platform," he said, "commits the American party unconditionally to the policy of slavery, to the iron dominion of the black power. I tell you, sir, I tell this convention, that we cannot stand upon this platform in a single free State of the North. The people of the North will repudiate it, spurn it, spit upon it. For myself, sir, I here and now tell you to your faces, that I will trample with disdain on your platform. I will not support it: I will support no man who stands upon it. Adopt that platform, and you array against you every thing that is pure and holy, every thing that has the elements of permanency in it, the noblest pulsations of the human heart, the holiest convictions of the human soul, the profoundest ideas of the human intellect, and the attributes of Almighty God. Your party will be withered and consumed by the blasting breath of the people's wrath. There is an old Spanish proverb, which says that 'the feet of the avenging deities are shod with wool.' Softly and silently these avenging deities are advancing upon you. You will find that 'the mills of God grind slowly;' but they grind to powder.

"Of a hundred and forty-two representatives of the free States of the North, a hundred and twenty, elected by more than three hundred thousand majority, are pledged against the Kansas-Nebraska iniquity. Your platform requires these representatives to violate their pledges to the people, to smother their own holiest convictions, to abandon your party, or resign their seats. Do you, sir, believe these representatives will obey your unholy decrees? Do you believe they will betray a free and generous people at your bidding? I tell you nay. They will trample with disdain upon your platform. They will spurn it, and spurn you. The people will sustain them, and trample your platform and you in the dust.

"Sir, the gentleman from Alabama (Judge Hopkins) takes exception to the declaration made by me the other day in reply to the gentleman from Virginia (Mr. Bolling), that 'the past was yours, the future ours.' He objects, he tells us, to my assuming the functions of a prophet. Sir, I make little pretensions to the gift of prophecy; but it requires but a slight knowledge of the aspects of the slavery question in America to pronounce the opinion, that the past of the republic belongs to slavery, the future to freedom. Perhaps the distinguished gentleman from Alabama believes that we of the North are mere conquered provinces; that the people will obey your decrees, and 'conquer their prejudices.' One year ago, when the slave propagandists proposed to repeal so much of the act of the 6th of March, 1820, as prohibited slavery in the vast territory lying in the heart of the continent, these slave propagandists laughed to scorn the predictions of the friends of freedom, that the repeal would meet the stern resistance of the people of the North. The haughty chiefs of the black power and the administration, and its Northern tools in Congress, have gone down before the stormy wrath of the people. The predictions made by us in the spring of 1854 are now historical deeds, 'consummated facts.' So it will be now. The deed you are about to perform will seal your doom forever.

"The antislavery sentiment of the North is a profound religious conviction, resting upon the commands of Almighty God to 'do unto others as we would that others should do unto us;' to 'love our neighbors as we love ourselves;' to 'undo the heavy burdens, and to let the oppressed go free.' Do you think that the descendants of the old sturdy Puritan race, that met the demands of priests, nobles, and kings, with the stern 'Thus saith the Lord,' will smother the holiest convictions of their souls, and obey the decrees of a body of men like this? I tell you, sir, that they will do so never."

Declaring himself in favor of relieving the Federal Government from all connection with and responsibility for slavery by its abolition in the District of Columbia, its prohibition in the Territories, and by the repeal of the Fugitive-slave Act, Mr. Wilson said, —

"Standing by Williams's slave-pen nineteen years ago, and gazing upon men, women, and children collected for the Southern markets, I pledged myself to liberty; and have never, in public or private, at home or abroad, spoken or written one word inconsistent with that pledge, and I never will do so to save any party at the command of any body of men on earth. When I united with the American organization in its hour of weakness, I told the men with whom I acted that my antislavery opinions were the matured convictions of years, and that I would modify or qualify my opinions or suppress my sentiments for no consideration on earth. From that hour to this, in public and in private, I have freely uttered my antislavery sentiments, and labored to promote the antislavery cause; and I tell you now, that I will continue to do so. You shall not proscribe antislavery principles, measures, or men, without receiving from me the most determined and unrelenting hostility. It is a painful thing to differ from our associates and friends; but when duty, a stern sense of duty, demands it, I shall do so.

"Reject this majority platform; adopt the proposition to restore freedom to Kansas and Nebraska, and to protect the actual settlers from violence and outrage; simplify your rules; make an open organization; banish all bigotry and intolerance from your ranks; place your movement in harmony with the humane progressive spirit of the age, — and you may win and retain power, and elevate and improve the political character of the country. Adopt this majority platform, commit the American movement to the slave perpetualists and the slave propagandists, and you will go down before the burning indignation and withering scorn of American freemen."

As usual in national conventions, the slave-power triumphed; and most of the Northern delegates left the council, and issued an address repudiating its action, and severing their connection with it.

Returning to Massachusetts, the delegates made a report to the State Council that had been called. Mr. Wilson and his associates urged that measures should be immediately taken to secure the united action of men of all parties who thought and felt alike upon the vital issues growing out of the aggressive policy of the slave-power. Here was another grand opportunity for unity and a combined opposition against the slave-masters; but it was fatally thrown away. The proposition to call a convention to organize such a party was rejected; and the high-raised expectation of the friends of liberty was again doomed to disappointment.

"I retired from that meeting," said Mr. Wilson, "with a sad heart, but with an unconquered soul." He continued to labor for unity of sentiment and action, and personally visited many leading Whigs, appealing to them to seize the occasion, to take the lead, in combining the people in one great party pledged to the policy of freedom. In a letter to Wendell Phillips, who had invited him to join in celebrating the anniversary of national independence at Framingham with the abolitionists, he wrote, —

"I hope that we shall all strive to unite and combine all the friends of freedom; that we shall forget each other's faults and shortcomings in the past, and all labor to secure that co-operation by which alone the slave is to be emancipated, and the domination of his master broken. Let us remember that more than three millions of bondmen, groaning under nameless woes, *demand* that we shall cease to reproach each other, and that we labor for their deliverance. To them that hallowed anniversary brings no ray of consolation, no beam of hope. To them the golden lustre of the sun illumes not their dark horizon. To them the golden thread of freedom is lost on earth. Let your friends, let all the friends of these wronged millions, strive to combine their efforts in practicable action for the advancement of the cause of the bondmen."

In July he visited the West, addressed the friends of liberty at Cincinnati, and a mass State convention in Indianapolis on the anniversary of the ordinance of 1787. In his speech at Indianapolis, which was received with strong expressions of gratification by the assembled thousands, he urged antislavery men, Americans, Whigs, and anti-Nebraska Democrats, to unite upon a common platform against the aggressions of slavery. As an antislavery man, he believed that the curse of God would rest on him if he did not strive to get men on such a platform. Referring to the American party, he said, that, as he understood it, it had wise and beneficent purposes in view. It was consistent with republicanism, with law, and with Christianity. "I loathe," he said, "the idea of opposition to foreigners as foreigners."

Returning to Massachusetts, Mr. Wilson attended the State Council that met at Springfield on the 7th of August. The committee on resolutions reported a proposition that the exigencies of the times required united political action, expressed a readiness to co-operate with others, and proposed the appointment of a committee, which, in conjunction with other committees, should call a State convention to nominate candidates to be supported at the ensuing election. But this proposition was sternly resisted; and a motion was made to strike out the words "to co-operate with," and insert the words "to invite the co-operation of." Mr. Wilson opposed this amendment, and advocated the original proposition in an elaborate speech.

"Sir," he said, "this amendment is ungenerous, unmanly, and unworthy of earnest, high-minded men. Let us who are in the majority be liberal and generous; let us meet the men of other organizations at least half-way; and let us extend the grasp of hands warm with the blood which courses through generous and manly hearts.

"I believe, Mr. President, that an immense majority of the people of Massachusetts are this day hungering and thirsting after that political union that shall bring together men whose hearts beat responsive to the tones of freedom. Sir, the instinctive sagacity of the people, wiser than the wisdom of political leaders, sees that by fusion alone can the people of the free States baffle the darling schemes of the chiefs of the black power. If fusion is defeated in Massachusetts, in the North, it will not be the work of the unselfish masses; but it will be owing to the selfish ambition and the criminal folly of political leaders. I warn the political chiefs of all parties against permitting their little petty interests, their unreasoning prejudices, to blind them to the great fact that the people want union, and *will have it through* your organizations, or *over* your organizations.

"If the representatives of the American party reject this proposition for fusion, I shall go home once more with a sad heart. But I shall not go home to sulk in my tent, to rail and fret at the folly of men: I shall go home, sir, with a resolved spirit and iron will, determined to hope on and to struggle on until I see the lovers of universal and impartial freedom banded together in one organization, moved by one impulse. For seven years I have labored to break up old organizations and to make new combinations, all tending to the organization of that great party of the future which is to relieve the government from the iron dominion of the black power.

"Sir, gentlemen may defeat this proposed fusion here to-day; but they cannot control the action of the people. A fusion movement will be made under the lead of gentlemen of the Whig, Democratic, and Free-soil parties, of talents and character. The movement will be in harmony with the people's movements in the North. Sir, such a movement will put a majority of the men who voted with you last autumn in a false position before the country, or drive them from your ranks. I cannot speak for others: but I tell you frankly, that I cannot be placed in a false position; I cannot, even for one moment, consent to stand arrayed against the hosts of freedom now preparing for the contest of 1856. I tell you frankly, that, whenever I see a formation in position to strike effective blows for freedom, I shall be with it in the conflict; whenever I see an organization in position antagonistic to freedom, my arm shall aid in smiting it down. While I shall be true to freedom, I shall not be false to the ideas which underlie the American movement. All my hopes for freedom, all my hopes for the triumph of those American ideas, are based wholly upon the united action of the people.

"These avowals are not inconsistent with my past avowals and acts. Never, since I became a member of the American organization, have I failed to utter my sentiments frankly in public and in private. By the unsolicited kindness of my friends, I have been assigned a position in the national councils. I say, unsolicited kindness: for, whatever might have been my desires or hopes, I never asked a single human being to vote for me; I never travelled a single mile or expended a single dollar to secure a vote. I see an eloquent gentleman present, who called upon me, while my election was pending, to request me to write something to modify my opinions upon slavery. He will remember that I stated fully my views upon that question: that I told him my opinions were the matured convictions of years; that I would not qualify them to win the loftiest position on earth; that I should carry them with me, if elected, into the Senate; and that, if the party with which I acted proved recreant to freedom, I would shiver it to atoms, if I had the power to do it. Chosen to represent Massachusetts in the national councils without the sacrifice of my antislavery opinions, I have acted, and I shall continue to act, up to these opinions."

The proposition had been made in the legislature to amend the Constitution by requiring a foreigner to reside in the country twenty-one years before he should be qualified to vote. To all attempts to sanction that proposition, and all other illiberal measures, Mr. Wilson gave a firm and persistent opposition.

"Sir," he said, "the American movement is not based upon bigotry, intolerance, or proscription. If there is any thing of bigotry, intolerance, or proscription, in the American movement, if there is any disposition to oppress or degrade the Briton, the Scot, the Celt, the German, or any one of another clime or race, or to deny to them the fullest protection of just and equal laws, it is time such criminal fanaticism was sternly rebuked by the intelligent patriotism of the state and country. I deeply deplore, sir, the adoption of the twenty-one-years amendment. It will weaken the American movement at home and in other States, especially in the West, and tend to defeat any modification whatever of the naturalization laws. I warn gentlemen who desire the correction of the evils growing out of the abuses of the naturalization laws against the adoption of extreme opinions. I tell you, gentlemen of the council, that this intense Nativism kills; yes, sir, it kills and is killing us, and, unless it is speedily abandoned, will defeat all the needed reforms the movement was inaugurated to secure, and overwhelm us all in dishonor. Every attempt, by whomsoever made, to interpolate with the American movement any thing inconsistent with the theory of our democratic institutions, any thing inconsistent with the idea that 'all men are created equal,' any thing contrary to the command of God's holy Word, that 'the stranger that dwelleth with you shall be unto you as one born among you, and thou shalt love him as thyself,' is doing that which will baffle the wise policy which strives to reform existing evils and to guard against future abuses."

All efforts for fusion proving unavailing, Mr. Wilson united with others in calling a mass convention, which assembled at Worcester, effected a union, and nominated Julius Rockwell for governor. He entered into the canvass with earnestness, and labored zealously in behalf of the nomination thus effected.

Although the attempts to exclude foreigners from holding office, and to require a residence of twenty-one years before voting, had failed, a proposition was carried through the legislature, and submitted to the people in May, 1859, requiring a residence of two years after naturalization. Mr. Wilson, who had opposed the other propositions, opposed this also, because it made "an invidious and offensive distinction against men who were born in other lands." To aid in its defeat, he presided at a public meeting in Faneuil Hall, which was addressed by the eminent German orator, Carl Schurz. On the 20th of April he addressed a letter to the Hon. Francis Gillette of Connecticut in opposition to the measure, in which he wrote as follows:—

"That there are great abuses growing out of the loose administration of the naturalization laws, especially in our large Atlantic cities and towns, all fair-minded men must admit. It has appeared to me that these admitted abuses could be remedied either by the modification or revision of the naturalization laws, or by a reform in their administration; and I have ever been ready in any practical mode consistent with the equal rights of all men to reform these acknowledged evils. But I have ever declared that I would support no measure, even to reform these abuses, which would in the slightest degrade any man, or class of men; that I would give to every human being equal rights,—the same equality I would claim for myself or my own son.

"No power on earth could force me to vote for any proposition which fair-minded and intelligent men felt to be unequal or personally degrading. Never have I supported any measure inconsistent with the equal rights of man; but, if I had ever unintentionally made such a mistake, I have nothing of that pride of consistency in regard to mere measures which would induce me to continue in the wrong because I had been wrong once. Better be right in the lights of to-day than be consistent with the errors of yesterday.

"For more than twenty years, I have believed the antislavery cause to be the great cause of our age in America,—a cause which overshadowed all other issues, state or national, foreign or domestic. In my political action I have ever endeavored to make it the paramount question, and to subordinate all minor issues to this one grand and comprehensive idea. It seems to me that the friends of a cause so vast, so sacred, should ever strive to save it from being burdened by the pressure of temporary interests and local and comparatively immaterial questions. With my comprehension of the transcendent magnitude of the issues involved in the solution of the slavery question in America, with the lights I have to guide my action, I should feel, if I put a burden on the antislavery cause by pressing the adoption of measures of minor importance, that I was committing a crime against millions of hapless bondmen, and should deserve their lasting reproaches, and the rebuke of all true and tried men who were toiling to dethrone that gigantic power which perverts the National Government to the interests of oppression."

This letter evoked a public reply from Hon. Amasa Walker, sharply criticising Mr. Wilson's opposition to the amendment. Under date of 2d of May, Mr. Wilson answered this letter, justifying his opposition, and vindicating the consistency of his action. In this letter he said, —

"I avowed at all times, while acting with the American organization, my readiness to remedy abuses growing out of the administration of naturalization laws by their revision; but I at all times announced my determination to vote for no proposition which would be unequal, unjust, or degrading, to any class of men.

"This was my position then: it is my position now. Then it required me to oppose, and I did oppose, the twenty-one-years proposition, the fourteen-years proposition, the proposition to make foreign-born citizens ineligible to office, the sending-out of the country men for the misfortune of poverty, and the reading-and-writing amendment: now it requires me to oppose the adoption of a proposition which simply makes a distinction between adopted and native-born citizens of the United States by requiring the adopted citizen to reside in the United States two years before he can exercise the right of suffrage, while it allows the native-born citizen to exercise that right after a residence of one year. I believe that the opinions of Republicans outside of Massachusetts upon this proposition approach unanimity. During the past five years, I have had some little opportunity to become acquainted with the public men of the Republican party from all sections of the country. I have, during those years, travelled in seventeen States, more than forty thousand miles, seen and counselled with the active men of the party, and addressed hundreds of thousands of the people. Few men have had better opportunities to become acquainted with leading men, and to know something of the opinions of the people; and I now say that I do not know a single Republican statesman, or a single Republican paper, or a single man in the rank and file of the Republican party, outside of Massachusetts, in favor of the adoption of this amendment."

Mr. Wilson was severely censured and sharply denounced for

his opposition to this measure. To these imputations he said, —

"I have no reply to make. Conscious that I have nothing personally to gain by these avowals of my opinions upon this question, and that I am actuated solely by a sincere desire to maintain the equal rights of American citizens, and to advance a cause my heart loves and my judgment approves, I am content to appeal from the impulsive censure of the present to the sober judgment of the future."

As Mr. Walker predicted in his letter, the people of Massachusetts ratified the two-years amendment by a decisive majority. It, however, remained in the Constitution but a brief period, and was stricken therefrom immediately after the opening of the Rebellion; thus giving the popular indorsement to Mr. Wilson's position.

CHAPTER VIII.

Thirty-third Congress. — Entrance into United-States Senate. — Douglas takes a Hand in a Small Game. — Benjamin F. Hallett to the Rescue on a Question of Veracity.

ON the tenth day of February, 1855, Henry Wilson the shoemaker took his seat in the Senate of the United States as the successor of Edward Everett the professor and diplomat, whose scholarship and oratory were of the highest order, and whose fame the State of Massachusetts had appropriated and lovingly cherished as part of her own. The difference between the new and the retiring senator, in opportunity, education, style of thought and expression, and in general political aims and principles, was one calculated to excite remark; and if among the scholars who adorn the classic precincts of Cambridge and Boston, or among the profound and learned jurists that grace the supreme bench of the State, there were those who had misgivings as to the propriety of the change, it is not matter for wonder. Mr. Everett was a man of highly-polished manners, great talents, and varied acquirements: but by some unaccountable mental eccentricity, or from his inclination to follow rather than lead in the political movements of the time, he had not kept even with the sentiment of the people of the State, and no longer represented their ideas on great questions that were impending; while Henry Wilson did represent those ideas. The question of propriety has since been settled by Wilson himself; and Mr. Everett, when he subsequently put himself in political accord with his successor, not only indorsed the propriety of the shoemaker's election, but did an act which counted more in saving his political reputation than any one act of his whole career. Mr. Wilson, it is true, was not so polished in manners and scholarship as Everett: few are: but neither was he deficient in material senatorial qualities. When Wilson entered the Senate, though Webster, Clay, and Calhoun were no longer there, it was still, as it is today, a body of great and distinguished men. John M. Clayton, Lewis Cass, Stephen A. Douglas. William H. Seward, Hannibal Hamlin, Charles Sumner, Hamilton Fish, Salmon P. Chase, Mason, Slidell, Hunter, and others, were among the men who were there, and in the prime of their powers and their fame. There was serious work near at hand, as was felt, but far more serious as it turned out. Franklin Pierce was president, Jeff. Davis in the cabinet, the Kansas question on their hands, and the whole administration, and all its ideas, sympathies, and devices, utterly at war with the spirit of the age, and utterly incompetent to the exigencies of the hour. It was the time for men like Wilson; only there were not enough of them. There were good men there to make thrilling speeches on the right side. But Wilson was more than a speech-maker: he was an organizer and a worker, — a man who could bring things to pass.

On the 21st of the month he made his *début* as a debater by a short speech announcing his intention to vote for measures proposing to reduce duties on imported articles which enter largely into the consumption of the masses.

Two days after, Feb. 23, the real career of Mr. Wilson as a senator of the United States was fairly commenced by a speech characteristic of the man, and which excited general attention, and, in certain quarters, a decided flutter. The occasion of the flutter was the introduction to notice of some resolutions on the slavery question, written by Mr. Hallett of Boston, and passed by the Democratic Convention Sept. 19, 1849. These resolutions were written for the local market of the State of Massachusetts, and not for national consumption, and they were flavored with sentiments on the slavery question that had become contraband and incendiary in Democratic circles in 1855. The first was in favor of "freedom and free soil wherever man lives throughout God's heritage;" and two of the others affirmed that slavery could not exist in the Territories without the sanction of Congress, — a doctrine which recent discoveries in political science had proved fallacious, and distasteful at Washington. Mr. Hallett being chairman of the National Democratic Committee at the time these resolutions were written, a great constitutional lawyer, and a high Democratic authority, their promulgation in the Senate with a full indorsement of soundness by the abolition agitator, Wilson, rendered the situation interesting.

Mr. Douglas was the first to comprehend the fatal tendency of the thrust Wilson had made at the vital point, and endeavored to break its force by insinuating that Wilson was a disunionist; that he had a letter written in Boston praising him, and asserting, that, upon the question of the dissolution of the Union, "he would prove himself a man." It was understood generally, that, when Stephen A. Douglas took any one in hand, there was occasion for it; and at such times the fur might be expected to fly in considerable quantities. In fact, Douglas was a power that many senators preferred to give a wide berth to; and a new-comer like Wilson, whom it was important to the dominant party to have crushed early, might naturally expect a demonstration from *him* to mean business. It was a time to try the courage, temper, and self-poise of any man; and the reply made on the instant was not only pertinent, but so manly and pointed, that Mr. Douglas was constrained to drop the subject, and watch for a more valuable place to make his attack. Wilson said,—

"All I have to say is, that I never uttered a word in my life to warrant such an assertion. Sir, I make no pretensions to any peculiar devotion to the Union over other men; but, if I know myself, I would sacrifice all of life and of hope to maintain and perpetuate the union of these States. From boyhood I have dreamed of a glorious destiny for my country. I have wished to see the flag of the Union wave in peaceful triumph over the North-American continent, over a confederacy of free commonwealths. I have so much faith in democratic ideas, so much confidence in the people, that I have no fears from the annexation of territory and the extension of the boundaries of the republic.

"The senator from Illinois (Mr. Douglas) has undertaken here to-night to denounce all of us of the North, whom he is pleased to call abolitionists, as disunionists. Now, sir, in my judgment, no part of the confederacy is more devoted to the Union than the State I have the honor, in part, to represent. I believe, that, in my State, the opinion in favor of the Union approaches unanimity. We respond with all our hearts to the words of Daniel Webster uttered on this floor more than twenty years ago, '*Liberty and union now and forever, one and inseparable.*' But we mean *liberty* and union. The voting antislavery men of Massachusetts will not be frightened from their advocacy of impartial liberty by threats, made here or elsewhere, to dissolve the Union. These menaces have no terrors for us. We know that the people will stand by the Union even if slavery should be abolished. . . .

"Now, sir, I assure the senators from the South that we of the free States mean to change our policy. I tell you frankly just how we feel, and just what we propose to do. We mean to withdraw from these halls that class of public men who have betrayed us and deceived you; men who have misrepresented us, and not dealt frankly with you. And we intend to send men into these halls who will truly represent us, and deal justly with you. We mean, sir, to place in the councils of the nation men who, in the words of Jefferson, 'have sworn on the altar of God eternal hostility to every kind of oppression of the mind and body of man.' Yes, sir, we mean to place in the national councils men who cannot be seduced by the blandishments, or deterred by the threats, of power; men who will fearlessly maintain our principles. I assure senators from the South that the people of the North entertain for them and their people no feelings of hostility; but they will no longer consent to be misrepresented by their own representatives, nor proscribed for their fidelity to freedom. This determination of the people of the North has manifested itself during the past few months in acts not to be misread by the country. The stern rebuke administered to faithless Northern representatives, and the annihilation of old and powerful political organizations, should teach senators that the days of waning power are upon them. This action of the people teaches the lesson, which I hope will be heeded, that political combinations can no longer be successfully made to suppress the sentiments of the people."

This style of language and thought was decidedly interesting to the Senate as then constituted: and the members somehow found themselves listening, and taking notes. Mr. Benjamin of Louisiana, an able lawyer and sharp fencer, rose, and acknowledged that the remarks of the new senator from Massachusetts were interesting, and desired to put a few questions, the pith of which was, whether Massachusetts would return fugitive slaves if the fugitive-slave act was repealed. Wilson promptly replied, that she would perform all her constitutional obligations, in his opinion. Then Mr. Rusk of Texas went at him, and Weller of California. But it was all of no use: he resolutely refused to get confused, or thrown from his balance; and finished his speech without sustaining damage, or perilling the reputation of his State.

This speech attracted so much attention, and the speaker escaped the claws of Douglas, Benjamin, Rusk, and Co. so absolutely without injury, that it was thought necessary to have something done about it; and, after an entire year of consideration, it was decided, that, if they could not squelch him in any other way, they might attempt to prove him a liar. Accordingly, Mr. Hallett carefully concocted a nice little pamphlet, raising against him a question of veracity; and it was printed in due form, and placed upon the tables of senators, with all proper authentication, and assumption of responsibility.

It is difficult now to understand the motives of Mr. Hallett in arraying himself against Henry Wilson on such a question and in such a way; for Mr. Hallett was not a fool, had generous instincts, and knew the man he assailed. In such an encounter there could be but one result, and that the reader will anticipate. Mr. Wilson said, —

"There has been placed, Mr. President, upon the desks of members of the Senate and House of Representatives, a pamphlet prepared by the author of these resolutions (Mr. Benjamin F. Hallett), now the United-States District Attorney for Massachusetts. Upon the titlepage of this pamphlet I find, in huge, staring capitals, these words: —

"'A Question of Veracity for Senator Henry Wilson!' Sir, this pamphlet, with this 'question of veracity for Henry Wilson' in large capitals upon its titlepage, is made up of extracts from a speech delivered by this government official at an administration meeting in Wilton, N.H., pending the late election. In this speech Mr. Benjamin F. Hallett has made a gross, wanton, and wholly unprovoked personal assault upon me. I say, sir, this assault is wholly unprovoked; for I have not, in the Senate or out of the Senate, in referring to or quoting from these resolutions, charged him with inconsistency, or uttered an unkind or disrespectful word towards him.

"But, sir, Mr. Benjamin F. Hallett has chosen to make this gratuitous personal assault upon me, and to thrust it into this chamber and into the other house. Sir, I shall promptly meet this assault. Mr. Benjamin F. Hallett raises 'a question of veracity for Senator Henry Wilson.' 'Senator Henry Wilson' here on the floor of the Senate, on this the twenty-first day of April, 1856, will settle this 'question of veracity,' raised for him by Mr. Benjamin F. Hallett, by demonstrating that Mr. Benjamin F. Hallett has made against me (in the pamphlet I hold in my hand) wholesale charges without the shadow of truth in them.

"Sir, Mr. Benjamin F. Hallett charges me with 'deliberate and repeated perversion' of these resolutions; with having 'falsified the record;' with having 'garbled and perverted' these resolves by 'quoting a single sentence, or a part of a resolution;' with having 'twice misquoted them in the Senate;' with having 'quoted detached sentences and half-sentences;' and with 'garbling and separating sentences.' Sir, these charges made by Mr. Benjamin F. Hallett I pronounce utterly and totally unfounded, without an element of truth in them. I never, in or out of the Senate, 'misstated' these resolutions; I never 'misquoted' them; I never 'perverted' them; I never 'quoted detached sentences' from these resolutions, or 'garbled' them by 'separating sentences.' Sir, I deny in the most emphatic language the truth of these wholesale charges; and, sir, I feel justified in applying to the author of these charges the language once applied to another by Burke, and to say that 'his charges are false, and he knows them to be false, and I know them to be false, and he knows that I know that he knows them to be false.'

"Sir, Mr. Benjamin F. Hallett graciously declares that he will not pronounce me 'a fool or a knave' for 'misquoting these resolutions,' as I 'may never have read them as a whole.' Sir, his gracious condescension is wholly misplaced. I assure him that my sins, if I have sinned, are not the sins of ignorance. Sir, I saw these resolutions in the hands of Benjamin F. Hallett on the morning of the 19th of September, 1849, in the cars between Boston and Springfield, and heard him read them to the Hon. Charles C. Hazewell, then associated with 'The Boston Times,' a gentleman of extraordinary memory and vast historical acquisitions. After he had finished reading these resolves, Mr. Hazewell asked him what 'the Southern Democrats would say to them.' Mr. Benjamin F. Hallett promptly replied, 'I don't care what they say. We have risked every thing for them. They deserted Gen. Cass, and elected Gen. Taylor. They may take care of themselves, and we will take care of ourselves.' Sir, I was present at the convention when they were reported by the author: so, sir, I know something of these resolves and their history; and I know, that, when they were penned, he was smarting under the defeat of 1848. He was also looking hopefully to a coalition with the Free-soilers in the ensuing State election. 'The Boston Post' (the office from which the pamphlet comes), edited then and now by Charles G. Greene, navy agent at Boston, on the 21st of September, in indorsing these resolutions (state and national), expressed the opinion that the two minority parties could act together in the pending election on State affairs.

"Mr. Benjamin F. Hallett charges me with having quoted 'garbled and disconnected *extracts* from the resolutions' in my speech of the 23d of February, 1855. He is prudently careful, sir, not to quote these 'garbled and disconnected extracts' as quoted by me in that speech. He did not do so for two reasons, — he did not wish to place them before the readers of this pamphlet; and, if he had quoted the extract in full from my speech, it would have been seen at once that I had not quoted three 'garbled and disconnected extracts,' but that I had quoted three whole, entire, complete resolutions, each embracing distinct, independent propositions. . . .

"And here, sir, I dismiss Mr. Benjamin F. Hallett to 'that sober and sagacious judgment of the people' which he invokes, — a judgment 'which never fails in the end to detect and detest' the man who makes unfounded accusations, or bears false witness against a political opponent."

We give this long extract, not for the purpose of reviving and perpetuating the unpleasantness of that day, nor for the desire to exult over the triumph of the senator, but to show the spirit that animated the Democratic leaders of the period, and with what antislavery men had to contend. The manner of the reply shows that Wilson was confident in his integrity, and in his ability to face the music, and give an account of himself that would not encourage another attack of the same character. He was at home to all comers on questions of veracity, and particularly to Benjamin F. Hallett.

At this session Mr. Wilson made a speech on the tariff in favor of a modification of duties, and said, "I think American labor will be best protected by taxing all the necessaries of life lightly, placing the raw materials which enter into our manufactures on the free list, raising revenue upon articles that come into competition with our manufactures, and upon the luxuries of life which are consumed by the more wealthy classes of society."

CHAPTER IX.

Thirty-fourth Congress. — Douglas and Wilson on Subduing. — Rusk on Fanaticism. — Brooks Challenges. — Central-American Affairs.

BY the middle of April, 1856, the Kansas question had grown into formidable proportions, and was before the Senate for debate and consideration. Douglas was on hand with his cunning scheme of popular sovereignty, which he fancied would meet the moderate men of all sections; but, in order to make it palatable to the advocates of slavery, he denounced with all the fierceness and ability at his command the friends of the Wilmot Proviso, calling them "black Republicans" and other opprobrious epithets, and threatened to "subdue them."

Wilson took up the gauntlet thus thrown down; met the great Illinois champion with good plain Saxon language, without any dodges or evasions, and in a style calculated to teach him that the present senators of Massachusetts were there for a purpose, and the days of compromises and child's play were approaching an end.

Mr. Douglas had made a reconnoissance the year previous to feel the mettle of his antagonist, and had reason to be satisfied that all his own resources would be needed to save the day; and he prepared for a vigorous conflict. Wilson was not unprepared, and in no mood to retreat.

Among other things he said, —

"The senator from Illinois may denounce us as black Republicans, as abolition agitators, if he thinks such language worthy of the Senate or of himself; but the issue is being made up in the country between the people and the slave propaganda. He told us the other day that he intended to subdue us. I say to that senator, We accept your issue. Nominate some one of your scarred veterans; some one who is committed, fully committed, to your policy. You want a candidate that is scarred with your battles. Well, sir, if he goes into the battle of 1856, he will not come out of it without scars. You have made the issue: put your chieftains at the head. No man fitter to lead than the honorable senator himself in this contest; for his position has the merit, at least, of being bold; and I like a bold, brave man who stands by his declarations. Now, I say to senators on the other side of the chamber, We will accept your issues. You may sneer at us as abolition agitators. That may have some little effect in some sections in the North, but very little indeed. We have passed beyond that. The people of this country are being educated up to a standard above all these little sneering phrases. We will accept your issue; but you will not, can not, subdue us. I tell the honorable senator he may vote us down, but subdue us never. We belong to a race of men that never were subdued; and, if anybody undertakes that work, he will find he has taken a rather costly contract. Subdue us! subdue us! Sir, you may vote us down; but we stand with the fathers. Our cause is the cause of human nature. The star of duty shines upon our pathway; and we will pursue that pathway, looking back for instructions to the great men who founded the institutions of the republic, looking up to Him whose 'hand moves the stars and heaves the pulses of the deep.' I tell the senator that this talk about subduing us and conquering us will not do. Gentlemen, you cannot do it. You may vote us down; but we shall live to fight another day. (Laughter.)

Mr. Douglas, —

> "He who fights and runs away
> May live to fight another day."

Mr. Wilson. — "We shall not run away to live: we shall live to run. (Laughter.) We shall go into the conflict in the coming contest like the Zouaves at Inkermann, with 'the light of battle on our faces.' If we fall, we shall fall to rise again; for the arm of God is beneath us, and the current of advancing civilization is bearing us onward to assured triumph.

"Now, I will tell you what we intend to do. We shall stand here and vote to defeat the bill reported by the senator from Illinois, because we believe, by the provisions of that bill, Kansas can be and will be invaded and conquered. We shall vote for the admission of this petition, for the admission of all petitions, from the people of Kansas; we shall vote for the admission of Kansas into this Union as a free State. If we fail, if you vote us down, we shall go to the country with that issue. We shall appeal to the people, to the toiling millions whose heritage is in peril, to come to the rescue of the people of Kansas, struggling to preserve their sacred rights. Madness may rule the hour; the black power, now enthroned in the National Government, may prolong for another Olympiad its waning influence: but we shall ultimately rescue the republic from the unnatural rule of a slaveholding aristocracy. Before the rising spirit of liberty this domination will go down."

The events of the last few years show how much nearer right Wilson was in his estimate of the course of events than his opponent. Kansas, instead of proving an ally of Democracy, became one of its most radical opponents, and helped to drive the malecontents to desperation and ruin.

On the 19th of December, 1856, Wilson made a strong speech on the president's message, and alluded to Mr. Rusk of Texas, who had spoken of Northern fanaticism, and asked if he supposed the people of the North were so stolid, ignorant, and deluded as to be deceived on a question of such magnitude.

Mr. Rusk. — "I do not know that I used the term 'fanaticism;' but I have frequently spoken of the slavery agitation, and I have as frequently expressed the conviction which is on my mind, that all the hue and cry about slavery is raised, not by the people of the North, not by the mechanics, not by the hard-fisted farmers, but by disappointed politicians who desire to get into office on a sectional issue."

Mr. Wilson. — "I hope the senator from Texas, and those who act with him, will disabuse their minds right speedily of that idea. Cast your eye over the North: take New England, with her hundred and fifty thousand popular majority against your candidate; take the great State of New York; take the whole line of Northern States; and, when you look at them, remember that we have a large plurality in all of them, except in a portion of them included within about forty thousand square miles of territory, and *that* we intend to burn over in the next four years. I allude to Eastern and Central Pennsylvania, Southern Indiana, Southern Illinois, and a small portion of New Jersey. There we mean to discuss the question, and have it well and clearly defined and understood. The rest of the North is ours. If you believe that the people are fanatics, or that their leaders deceive them, remember one thing, — that in 1850 there were in the United States nearly eight hundred thousand free persons above twenty years of age who could not read nor write. Only ninety-four thousand out of this eight hundred thousand happen to live in the States which Frémont has carried. Remember another thing, — that the State of Massachusetts, which you consider so ultra, a people so easily deluded, prints within a few thousand and circulates more newspapers within the State than all the fifteen Southern States of the Union. Remember they have more volumes in their public libraries than all the slave States. Remember they give away more money to the Bible and Missionary and other benevolent societies every year than the entire slaveholding States; and they have done so during the last quarter of a century.

"I tell you, sir, that the people are ahead of us; and that is what you fear. You say that they are deceived by us; and then you turn round, and declare that you cannot rely on our disclaimers, because the people will pass beyond the direction and control of political leaders. The people understand this question, sir: they know their responsibilities, their powers, and their duties.

"The senator from South Carolina (Mr. Butler) boasted of the great contentment among the slaves in his section of the Union. He told us that slaves who had run away were returning to their masters, and that this was the best kind of fugitive-slave law. Perhaps the senator is right; but the events transpiring all over the South hardly sustain the senator's declarations. I commend to him, whenever he boasts on this floor of the contentment of the bondman, the words of Edmund Burke: 'He who makes a contented slave makes a degraded man.'

"Look at the condition of affairs in your section of the Union to-day. In many places your people think they have found evidences of incipient rebellions. The supporters of Buchanan and Fillmore have rivalled each other in misrepresenting the sentiments, principles, and policy of the supporters of John C. Frémont. The leaders of the Southern Democracy have everywhere denounced the Republican party as a party in favor of emancipation by the exercise of the powers of the Federal Government. The hungry ear of these bondmen drank in these false accusations and unjust reproaches. Your words will be to them a possession forever, exciting hopes that will never die. Go home. Undeceive those whom you have deceived. Do us justice. Place us where we are, and where we intend to stand, — opposed to slavery everywhere, in favor of its abolition everywhere; opposed to the domination of the slave-power, but conceding to the people of the slave States their constitutional rights to settle the matter in their own time and in their own way.

"Senators desired to know how we should vote on the admission of Kansas as a slaveholding State. I answer for myself: If Kansas applies for admission as a slave State, I will reply in the words of Caleb Cushing, the law officer of this government. In arguing the question of the admission of Arkansas, he said, speaking in regard to the power of Congress over the subject, —

"'The Constitution confers upon us the discretion to admit new States at will. It limits, in certain respects, our power to act affirmatively; but it does not limit in any respect our discretion, on the negative side, of a refusal to admit new States.'

"Resting upon this authority of the distinguished legal adviser of the administration, I will answer your question, whether I will vote for the admission of Kansas as a slave State, in his words: —

"'I do not persuade myself that liberty is an evil, or that slavery is a blessing. When called upon to accord my official sanction to a form of government which not merely permits, but expressly perpetuates, slavery, I should be false to all the opinions and principles of my life if I did not promptly return a peremptory and emphatic *No!*'

"The senator from Texas commends our devotion to the Union. We have ever supported the Union; and I tell you, sir, what we intend to do in regard to its support. The senator from Pennsylvania the other day denounced the Barnwell Rhett school of politicians. I suppose he thought it safe to attack that little squad of fanatics, as he calls them, in South Carolina. But, sir, we, the Republicans, do not confine our denunciations to that little faction. We denounce your Governor Wises, all your chosen leaders who have threatened to destroy the Union if the fortunes of the election went against them, — the men who have your confidence, — the men who go to Wheatland, and have the ear of your incoming executive. I give you notice to-day, gentlemen, what we intend to do. If the incoming administration sends into this body the nomination of a single man who ever threatened the dissolution of the Union, we intend to camp on this floor, and to resist his confirmation to the bitter end. I give you notice now that we shall resist the coming into power of all that class of men as enemies of the Constitution and the Union."

In May, 1856, Preston S. Brooks of South Carolina made the brutal assault upon Mr. Sumner for words spoken in debate, and not personal, which startled the free States, and awoke them to a realizing sense of the approach of an era of blood. Mr. Wilson assisted in conveying his colleague to his lodgings, and the next day brought the matter before the Senate in a brief and appropriate manner, denouncing the act as "a brutal, murderous, and cowardly assault." It seems strange now that any one should have been in a frame of mind to doubt the propriety of Wilson's words; but Butler of South Carolina and others raised a point of order, and Brooks himself a point of honor, — in those days it was so difficult for a Southerner to get out of order, and so easy for a Northern man. Brooks sent a challenge to Wilson, which he declined, but repeated the objectionable words, declared he thought them true, refused to retract, and stated his firm and religious belief in the right of self-defence. The manly letter declining from principle to fight a duel was fully approved by the Northern people, and had a strong influence in abrogating the barbarous fashion of duelling then in vogue at Washington.

Burlingame, it is true, accepted a challenge from Brooks, but on terms that operated in the same way to render the practice unpopular. The duel having been declined by Wilson, there were threats of retaliation by the chivalry; but they were not executed, and Wilson was not deterred from speaking his mind and getting out of order as usual. He addressed the Senate upon the subject on the 13th of June, and gave Senator Butler a "dressing" such as the arrogant slavocrats were not accustomed to, and vindicated Mr. Sumner most triumphantly. This was a time to try a man's pluck and ability; and it is proper to say that Massachusetts was worthily represented and vindicated. Mason of Virginia, one of the most arrogant men ever in the Senate, afterwards so prominent in the "Mason and Slidell" affair, came in for a first-rate notice in this speech. Wilson said, —

"The senator from Virginia, not now in his seat (Mr. Mason), when Mr. Sumner closed his speech, saw fit to tell the Senate that his hands would be soiled by contact with ours. The senator is not here: I wish he were. I have simply to say that I know nothing in that senator, moral, intellectual, or physical, which entitles him to use such language towards members of the Senate, or any portion of God's creation. I know nothing in the State from which he comes, rich as it is in the history of the past, that entitles him to speak in such a manner. I am not here to assail Virginia: God knows. I have not a feeling in my heart against her or against her public men. But I do say it is time these arrogant assumptions ceased here. This is no place for assumed social superiority, as though certain senators held the keys of cultivated and refined society. Sir, they do not hold the keys, and they shall not hold over me the plantation-whip.

"I wish always to speak kindly towards every man in this body. Since I came here, I have never asked an introduction to a Southern member of the Senate, — not because I have any feelings against them (for God knows I have not); but I knew that they believed I held opinions hostile to their interests, and I supposed they would not desire my society. I have never wished to obtrude myself on their society, so that certain senators could do with me as they have boasted they did with others, — refuse to receive their advances, or refuse to recognize them on the floor of the Senate. Sir, there is not a coolie in the guano islands of Peru who does not think the Celestial Empire the whole universe. There are a great many men who have swung the whip over the plantation who think they not only rule the plantation, but make up the judgment of the world, and hold the keys not only to political power, as they have done in this country, but to social life.

"The senator from South Carolina assails the resolutions of my State with his accustomed looseness, as springing from ignorance, passion, prejudice, and excitement. Sir, the testimony before the House committee sustains all that is contained in those resolutions. Massachusetts has spoken her opinions: and, although the senator has quoted 'The Boston Courier' to-day (and I would not rob him of any consolation he can derive from that source). I know Massachusetts; and I can tell him, that, of the twelve hundred thousand people of Massachusetts, you cannot find in the State one thousand — administration office-holders included — who do not look with loathing and execration upon the outrage upon the person of their senator and the honor of their State. The sentiment of Massachusetts, of New England, of the North, approaches unanimity. Massachusetts has spoken her opinions. The senator is welcome to assail them if he chooses; but they are on the record. They are made up by the verdict of her people; and they understand the question, and from their verdict there is no appeal."

During this Congress Wilson made many other speeches, giving his views upon opening the public lands to actual settlers, — a scheme he strongly favored, on his usual theory of giving working-men a chance to get homes without paying a bonus to speculators, — on the Clayton-Bulwer Treaty, and in favor of the Monroe doctrine.

We give one short extract to show the nature of his ideas on these subjects: —

"I would take care of our interests in Central America: I would let Great Britain alone there, and leave it to her to commence an aggressive policy if she chooses so to do; and, if she does commence such a contest, it should never close until the power of England on the North-American continent is forever broken, and we are left in possession of North America to the polar regions, where civilization is arrested by the barriers of perpetual frost.

"I say then, sir, that the only way, in my judgment, to get out of our present embarrassment, is to declare the Clayton-Bulwer Treaty null and void; to negotiate in Central America for the protection of our transit-routes across that country. The abrogation of the treaty does not lead to war. It is the policy which will, in my judgment, promote the future peace and interest of the country. I would vote against the Clayton-Bulwer Treaty if it were before us to-day; for I can never agree to make an arrangement with England, or any other foreign power, that we will not exercise dominion over any portion of this continent. I have no sympathy with the policy that would extend the boundaries of the republic by lawless violence; but I have faith in democratic institutions. I believe, that, wherever the jurisdiction of this country extends on this continent, the interests of humanity will be ultimately promoted by it. Agreeing with the doctrine laid down by Mr. Everett in his admirable letter upon the tripartite treaty, I would never bind ourselves by any treaty obligations that we will not annex, if we and the people who live in the territory desire it, any portion of this continent."

CHAPTER X.

Thirty-fifth Congress. — Facts for Gwin. — Committees. — Running Debates. — Predictions and more Facts. — Thirty-sixth Congress.

AT the commencement of the Thirty-fifth Congress, the Democrats felt a strong inclination to curb the growing influence of the Republican party, and deprive it of all possible chance to interfere with the will and schemes of the administration, especially in relation to the Kansas, slavery, and commercial questions. One of the ways to accomplish this was to exclude from the committees as many Republican senators as possible and maintain any show of fairness and decency: but, it being determined to strike pretty deep in this direction, an excuse or pretence which would justify was thought desirable; and Mr. Gwin of California was put forward to make it. He was very much astonished that the other side should make any complaints, "because it is but recently in the history of the country that the party to which those gentlemen belong obtained control of the other House, though in a minority there. And how did they arrange its committees? There never was a more flagrant partisan character given to the committees of a legislative body, and they were never more sectional."

The moment Mr. Gwin concluded, Wilson was on his feet, and at once began to pile in his inexorable facts against the assertions of the California senator. He said,—

"I believe the honorable senator from California said the committees were never more unfairly constituted than at the last Congress, when the Republicans obtained possession of the House by an accident. Now, sir, I hold in my hand an analysis of the committees of the House of last year. There were upon those thirty-seven committees a hundred and thirty-one Republicans and a hundred and three of the opposition. The committees were constituted almost invariably of five Republicans to four opposition. The chairmanship of several of these committees was given to the supporters of the administration. The chairmanship of the Committee on Military Affairs, certainly one of the most important committees in either House, was given to Gen. Quitman of Mississippi. No man has a right to complain of the organization of the committees of the House of Representatives by the speaker last year. He was not only just, but liberal, towards the opposition. He gave four opposition members to five Republicans on the Committee of Ways and Means. The Committee on Commerce was constituted of a majority of the opposition, the numbers being four Republicans to five opposition. The Committee on Public Lands had five Republicans to four opposition; and the committees on the Post Office, the District of Columbia, the Judiciary, Indian Affairs, the Military, and Foreign Affairs, were constituted in the same proportions. The Committee on Territories was the only one constituted, as the senator from California says is the usual Democratic practice, six to three. The Committee on Patents stood three to two; while the Committee on the Library had a majority of the opposition, having consisted of one Republican to two opposition. The record will bear to all time the evidence of the fairness and liberality of Speaker Banks and of the Republican party.

"My friend from Michigan (Mr. Chandler) has said that the time may come when the Republicans may have a majority on this floor, and what you mete out to us shall be meted out to you. I cannot concur with my friend in that remark. I trust, sir, that we shall have a majority on the floor of this Senate; I have no doubt the time is to come when the men who oppose slavery and its power will have it: but, when that time comes, I trust the committees of this body will be liberal, just, and national in every respect; and that we shall not only be just, but liberal, towards those who are unjust and illiberal towards us. . . .

"An analysis of these committees has been made by the senator from Maine (Mr. Hamlin). Reference has been made to the Committee on Commerce by the senator from Wisconsin (Mr. Doolittle). Sir, it is well known that the protest was made last March, in this chamber, against the organization of the Committee on Commerce. It was believed, and declared on this floor, that the Committee on Commerce was organized so as to prevent river and harbor improvement bills from being reported. I have no objection to the senators who compose that committee. The senator from Alabama (Mr. Clay), the chairman of it, comes from a State largely, almost wholly, engaged in agricultural pursuits, having but thirty-six thousand tons of the five million tons of shipping of the United States. The senator from Georgia (Mr. Toombs), coming from a State that has twenty-nine thousand tons of shipping out of the five millions, is on that committee. The senator from North Carolina (Mr. Reid), coming from a State that has sixty thousand tons of shipping out of five million tons, is also a member of that committee. These three agricultural States, having only a hundred and twenty-five thousand tons of shipping, have three members of this committee; while the great State of New York, with a million five hundred thousand tons of shipping, and the North-western States bordering on the Great Lakes, are not represented on it at all. The senator from Louisiana (Mr. Benjamin) is upon the committee, and I think fitly there, representing as he does a State located at the mouth of the Mississippi River, and largely interested in commerce. We were given to understand last year that these errors should be corrected; and yet the correction has not been made. Four of the members of the Naval Committee are from the Southern States, — States which have neither commerce, ships, nor seamen. . . .

"For one, I do not complain of our positions on these committees. I take it we are all satisfied; that we care very little about these positions. We complain of the sectional character of the committees. That they are sectional, everybody must admit. Why is not some chairmanship assigned the senator from Ohio (Mr. Pugh), certainly one of the ablest supporters here of the administration, of the majority of this chamber? Take the twelve or thirteen important committees of this body, the only committees that are of any importance in the body, and but two are presided over by Northern men. The organization of this chamber, the organization of the government in each and every department, is proslavery But I do not know that we should complain; for the fact now stands clearly revealed to the gaze of mankind, that the present Democratic party and the proslavery party of this country are the same. The history of the one during the past twenty years must ever be the history of the other."

During the first session of 1858, the Minnesota and Kansas bills for admission were frequently before the Senate for discussion, and often there were little running commentaries, explanations, questions, answers, and retorts interjected at intervals during the delivery of the set speeches; and it is in these little sudden and unlooked-for encounters that men exhibit their real knowledge and accuracy, rather than in the carefully-prepared speeches which may be crammed for the occasion, and a large portion of the valuable facts forgotten in a week after delivery. In these spurts of cross-firing Wilson was frequently engaged, and displayed a surprising amount of ready and important information having a bearing on the question or on the course of remark.

Thus, when Mr. Brown of Mississippi objected to a provision for taking the votes of civilized Indians, Wilson retorted by saying that he should remember that the dominant party, to which Brown belonged, obtained their ascendency in the Territory of Minnesota by the votes of uncivilized Indians; that at one voting-place there was a large collection of the savages, and an Indian agent having some spare articles of clothing would go out and robe a few of them, bring them in, and have their votes deposited; then take them back, and strip them to use the same garments on another lot; and this process was carried on all day, and a large vote taken.

In some of these speeches he would give statistics of the population of States and sections at different periods, the relative gain and loss, the number of emigrants and States from which they went; and various things of that character.

On one occasion Mr. Benjamin of Louisiana was tripped by our senator on some small point, and testily replied that he was "utterly tired and sick of discussing the question on the asseverations of gentlemen as to what appeared in the newspapers, or what people told them. I look at the record in my hand, and not at what is told me outside, nor at newspaper partisan statements." Now, that was very good for Mr. Benjamin, sick and tired, and, on the whole, an improvement on the antagonist who copied from a paper in his "t'other jacket-pocket," as related in a former chapter; but Wilson knew about records and authorities, and Mr. Benjamin was met in a fashion not calculated to relieve his weariness or cure his complaint. Said Mr. Wilson, —

"Mr. President, in reply to what seems to me to be rather an extraordinary remark of the senator from Louisiana, that some senators were accustomed to bring into the Senate what has appeared in the public press: now, I have sent for 'The Daily Globe,' and I find the statement I made verified. This ordinance appears at the head of the Constitution as published there, and so appeared at the same time in the Territory of Kansas. Mr. Calhoun himself testifies that it was voted for as a part of the Constitution by the people. Although the senator from Missouri has told us that the people did not vote upon the Constitution at all, Mr. Calhoun testifies that they did, and voted for this ordinance as a part of the Constitution.

"I wish to say to the senator from Louisiana that I have no contempt for the public press of this country. I have fully as much respect for what appears in the public press as I have for what appears in manufactured official papers. I will examine the statements of the public press to see whether they be correct, as I will examine what appears in official papers and see if they be correct. The one can state falsehoods; and we all know the other does. I desire to say to the senator from Louisiana, that, when I make a statement on this floor, I intend to make it on what I believe to be good authority; and that senator knows, that, with all his ingenuity, he has never yet been able to show the mistakes or the misstatement of any assertions of fact which I have made here."

At one time Mr. Pugh of Ohio endeavors a corner in this fashion:—

Mr. PUGH.—"Will the senator allow me to make a suggestion?"

Mr. WILSON.—"Certainly."

Mr. PUGH.—"I understand the senator complains of the convention act of 1857, because it was designed to cut off the spring emigration of that year. Am I right?"

Mr. WILSON.—"Yes, sir."

Mr. PUGH.—"Then why does the senator complain that the spring emigration of 1855 voted? It is as broad as it is long."

Mr. WILSON.—"I will state the difference. This act provided for the taking of the census in March or April. Then the names were to be placed in the hands of officials to make up the registration. This was to be done in May; and a residence of six months was required to entitle a man to vote. It cut off the thousands who went there as actual residents in March, April, May, and the first three weeks in June,—men who were to cast their fortunes in the Territory. The four thousand nine hundred men who went over from Missouri in 1855 went back the next day; marched back with banners and music: they were not, and did not intend to be, residents. That is the difference. I hope the senator from Ohio sees it."

As the senator from Ohio made no further remark, it is to be inferred that he did "see it."

Mr. Brown, of Mississippi, thought Wilson made too many old speeches, and said he preferred old wine to old speeches. Wilson, in reply, said, "I will call the senator's attention to one of *his* old speeches; and I commend him to the study of old speeches, especially his own old speeches. I like my old speeches, because I intend they shall be so sound in principle, correct in sentiment, and accurate in facts, that I can refer to them with safety." He then went on to prove that Mr. Brown opposed the admission of California as a State because it would destroy the balance between the slave and free States. "What!" he exclaimed, "a balance between the North and the South! a balance between the seventeen millions of Northern freemen and the seven millions of Southern freemen! a balance between the minority and the majority of the country! The whole doctrine is anti-democratic, is local, is sectional, in all its aspects, and should be scouted from this chamber and from the country, as at war with our republican institutions and our republican ideas." Yes, indeed! How plain and clear to Henry Wilson! but how hard to beat into the brains of Albert G. Brown, Jefferson Davis, Judah P. Benjamin, and their Northern allies and followers!

Wilson was terribly in earnest

on the Kansas question, and threw his whole soul into it; working day and night with an energy and perseverance that would kill outright many who are regarded as great workers. He collated the facts, and flung them into the face of every senator who attempted to darken counsel, falsify the record, and mislead the people. Mr. Brown attempts to make it appear that the Boston Emigrant-aid Society was at the bottom of certain troubles, that this society was instigated by a congressional circular, and that it is abolition interference in that form which stirs up the strife; and Wilson meets him by showing that the Aid Society was organized several months before the date of the circular. Brown complains that the society had a charter, with a capital of five million dollars, of which only twenty thousand could be used in Massachusetts; and Wilson shows that the society never organized under that charter at all. Mr. Brown thought there was nothing very wrong in the election of March 30; and Wilson replies by showing that there were only fourteen hundred residents in the Territory who voted that day: that seven hundred were free-State men: and that between eight and nine hundred slave-State votes were cast in the town of Lawrence alone by men from Missouri, who went in there for that purpose, and went out when the voting was over. To back up some suspicious statement, a paper was read, signed by one Henry Clay Pate, which Wilson examines, and tells the senator, that, in eleven lines of it, there are "twelve absolute lies," — as plain language, certainly, as any used by "Truthful James," or any other promulgator of information in later times. And now comes up his old idea, so long indulged, and so ardently labored for, — a union of parties with live ideas. "I think there will soon be a general union in the North as there now is in the South: we are fast coming to it. And let me tell the senators on the administration side of this chamber, that if they consummate, if they support, — whether they succeed or not, — the bringing of Kansas into the Union under the Lecompton Constitution, with a knowledge of all these monstrous frauds scattered over the land, comprehended by the whole country, they will do more to unite all honest, liberty-loving, God-fearing men in the North than has been accomplished by any act ever adopted by this government. Your Kansas-Nebraska policy shivered to atoms the great Whig party, which had battled, sometimes successfully, for power here, under the lead of some of the most accomplished statesmen of the country. Another party sprang up, — the American party. It paused, it faltered, and it went down under the general judgment of the people of the free States. The Republican party rose in one year from a few thousand men, and gave at the last presidential election a million three hundred and forty thousand votes. It came much nearer than you wished taking the control of this government, of this country. The opinions they entertain, the policy they avow, the sentiments that swell their bosoms, are deepening and spreading all over the land. Those opinions and sentiments will unite the Northern people. Those sentiments and opinions cannot be hemmed in by lines of latitude and longitude. They will yet be adopted by fair-minded and honorable men everywhere who love their country, who love justice and liberty; and, whenever anybody shall raise the black flag of slavery and disunion in the South, he will find leaping from the ranks of the people thousands of patriotic men who will stand by the government and defend it." Very much so, Mr. Wilson; but all do not see it yet.

On the 17th of April, 1858, Wilson made a short speech in favor of postponing action on the Pacific Railway Bill until December, on the ground that the government was in debt, the people were in debt; and while roads could not pay, or routes like the one from Portland to Montreal, there was no chance of one paying to San Francisco. At the same time he was strongly in favor of the road, and regarded it as a necessity.

May 8, 1858, he addressed the Senate upon the death of Judge Evans, a member from South Carolina, in language of feeling eloquence appropriate to the occasion, closing as follows: "He will soon rest, Mr. President, beneath the soil of his own native State, which he loved so well, and served so faithfully. That State has given to the councils of the republic many not undistinguished sons; but the sods which will lie on his bosom will press the heart of as pure, as conscientious, as honest a public servant as she ever gave to the service of the nation. Let the people of his native South Carolina, let the personal friends who have known him so long and loved him well, let the sorrowing mourners around his now-clouded hearthstone, be cheered in this hour of affliction with the assurance that we the representatives of sister commonwealths, we his associates and friends in this chamber, will ever revere his name, and cherish his memory with affectionate regard."

The speech of Mr. Wilson on the fishing bounties, May 12, 1858, was one of the best ever made on that subject. It was earnest, and crowded with facts. He tells them that his constituents have half the vessels, half the capital, and half the number of persons, engaged in the cod-fishery in the country; that, at the opening of the Revolution, half the importations into the country were paid for by the fisheries of Massachusetts; that the policy of England concerning them was one of the causes of the Revolution; that John Adams and Thomas Jefferson and John Quincy Adams thought that to foster the fisheries as a nursery of navigation was one of the landmarks of the government of the United States. Mr. Mallory of Florida having said that Massachusetts fishermen did not make good sailors and soldiers, Wilson told him that the crew of the old "Constitution," which performed such wonders in the war of 1812, came from Essex County, Mass.; and to that war Marblehead, with only thirteen hundred polls, sent an entire regiment of soldiers. These things from the reading of Squire Eastman's seven hundred books.

To those senators from the South who opposed bounties to the fishermen because they were a local interest, Wilson said that the whole amount of bounties would not exceed a hundred and fifty thousand dollars; and yet we paid not less than twelve million dollars annually in duties on sugar for the sole benefit of a few hundred planters in Lousiana, besides paying them fifty thousand dollars in the way of seeds; that the State of Massachusetts paid annually her own postage, and two hundred and fifty-two thousand dollars towards the general expenses for postage, while the State of Louisiana did not pay her postage within five hundred and twenty-three thousand dollars. And so he went on pouring out facts and figures to show how much Massachusetts did, how little she asked for, and how important the fisheries are to the commerce and navy of the nation.

The John Brown raid is no longer a source of excitement; but it is a subject of deep interest, and ever will be. In 1859, however, it was different; and many persons in and out of Congress had the idea that Brown had done a deed which would forever make his name infamous, and politically extinguish any public man who was charitable enough to the old veteran to call him crazy. When Congress met in December, one of the first moves of the Democrats was to annihilate Wilson by connecting him with the affair; and A. G. Brown came forward prepared to do the work, which seemed easy. To this end he produced a resolution passed at a public meeting in Natick, Nov. 20, in these words: "*Resolved*, That it is the right and duty of the slaves to resist their masters, and the right and duty of the people of the North to incite them to resistance, and aid them in it." He charged that Wilson was present at this meeting, which was a meeting of his friends; and desired to know whether he in any mode opposed or resisted its passage. Wilson said he was present at the meeting as a spectator, but took no part, and that probably not more than twenty persons voted on the question; that it was well known in Massachusetts that he did not approve of John Brown's raid. He was in favor of free discussion, however; and often went to meetings with whose objects he did not sympathize.

Mr. Brown subsided upon this: but the press continued to harp upon it until the rebel raid upon Fort Sumter; but, since then, John Brown's soul has marched on without serious molestation.

On the 25th of January, 1860, Wilson addressed the Senate in an elaborate speech, able, pungent, and, as usual, crowded with facts. In this speech he undertook to show that rebellion was meditated by the South if they failed to carry the election; and, to sustain his points, he quoted from Southern papers the utterances of public men. One of these, by Senator Iverson of Georgia, that gentleman denied; but his action afterward shows that his denial was of little worth. He admitted, however, that he did say, "Slavery must be maintained in the Union, if possible; out of it, if necessary; peaceably if we may, forcibly if we must." Wilson thought this declaration incapable of more than one construction; and he went on at great length in a manner that stirred the sensibilities of the Democratic leaders most profoundly. They were playing a double game; plotting treason, but doing it in the guise of champions of the Union: and, as Wilson's speech stripped off the mask and exposed their schemes, they feared its effect in the pending election; and so Mr. Clingman, one of their most eloquent orators, and Jefferson Davis, their ablest statesman, came to the rescue. Mr. Davis, strange to say, was not a disunionist; he had been misunderstood; he only meant to leave when the Constitution should be destroyed.

In January, 1860, there was a running debate between Wilson and the two senators from South Carolina in relation to the expulsion of Mr. Hoar from that State. Chesnut and Hammond alleged that South Carolina enacted the law, which Samuel Hoar, father of Judge Hoar and George F. Hoar, was contesting, because Massachusetts had excited slaves to insurrection, or committed some act of aggression: and Wilson showed that the law was enacted in 1820, long before the abolition excitement; that it was held unconstitutional by William Wirt, then United-States Attorney-General, and Judge Johnson of South Carolina, of the Supreme Court of the United States. Hammond said he was governor when Mr. Hoar came to Charleston; that he had known him in Congress as a mild, pleasant old gentleman, and not incendiary at all; and he took care that he wasn't hurt, and in a friendly way invited him to leave. The aggression of Massachusetts consisted in sending him there. Why did she not employ a lawyer in Charleston? Wilson said she did endeavor to; but no one would undertake the case. The way these senators were driven to the wall compelled the strong men of the South to come to the rescue; and Jeff. Davis again entered the lists, and made a long, able, and interesting speech, in the course of which he quoted and eulogized Caleb Cushing, and defended Democracy. On the 10th of April, in reply to Mason of Virginia, who had said the colored people in the North were deteriorating, Wilson said, "I disagree with the senator from Virginia altogether. In my State we have between eight and nine thousand colored people: and I say here to-day, they are intelligent; that they universally attend our schools; they can read and write; they are industrious; and I may say, that, in intelligence and personal character, they are little if any inferior to the average of the population of my State or the country." He announced his intention at some future time to present statistics to prove that they were not tending to barbarism; that they had made progress in the last quarter of a century; spoke of the thirteen hundred free colored people of Washington as orderly, law-abiding, and increasing in intelligence.

Mason, in his reply, made allusion to Massachusetts in a way that goes far to explain how utterly such men misunderstood things. He said, "I remember very well when I really had the good fortune to be in the State which the honorable senator represents, — Massachusetts; that riding through the beautiful country adjacent to Boston, appropriated to villas, magnificent country-seats of hospitable, kind, and generous gentlemen, as far as my intercourse went with them, evincing accumulated wealth displayed in beautiful taste, I was struck with the fact, that, in three out of four of their most beautiful and highly-adorned grounds opening upon the public highway, there was not a gate; and all the preserves of flowers and shrubbery, and all that which required attention, and to be saved from depredation, were open to the highways; and, wherever there was a gate (and they were very few), I never saw the gate shut.

"I was struck with the fact, and remarked to a gentleman, 'How is this? No means whatever to keep off the depredations of cattle who are allowed to roam at large?' — 'Why,' said he, 'that is not allowed;' and, in all my ride, I never saw even a goat or pig upon the highway anywhere." (Here comes the point of the joke.) "Well, but," said I, "in my country, and all through the South, the really poor people pasture their milch-cows on the highways (and very good pasture they get); and their other stock run upon the public roads, and are not molested."

That was Senator Mason's idea of prosperity and a happy condition of society, set forth as a contrast for the benefit of Senator Wilson, who knew all about poverty. Just fancy Henry Wilson, or any other Yankee, emigrating to Virginia for the sake of living in a country where pigs and goats obtain free pasture on the public highways! Poor Mr. Mason could not enjoy his ride with no pigs in sight!

April 12, 1860, Wilson introduced an act to grant a million acres of public land to the cities of Washington and Georgetown for a school-fund. The proposition to do any thing for education in the District of Columbia troubled the patriotism of Jeff. Davis. He called it "a cheap humanity," and lectured the Massachusetts senator soundly. In his reply, Wilson said, "The senator says I had better look in my own neighborhood, to my neighbors and friends. I do look to them; and I say at home and abroad, at all times and on all occasions, wherever I can give a vote to lighten the burdens of a human being, that vote shall be given. I give it at home; I give it here; I give it everywhere. It is not the first time we have heard remarks made here about a movement in my State called a 'strike.' Let me tell senators they do not understand it. Men are on a strike in my State and town today that own the houses they live in. They are not satisfied with the prices paid; they want more; they have a right to demand more; and I sympathize with them in their efforts to obtain better prices for their work. . . . If political partisans, or men who predict the failure of free society, hope to make any thing by the movement of the shoemakers of Massachusetts, they are destined to be sadly mistaken."

And they were mistaken.

CHAPTER XI.

Debate with Senator Hammond. — Mud-sills.

IN 1830 Massachusetts and South Carolina met by their representatives on the floor of the Senate in an intellectual and moral encounter that will long be held memorable by the people of the United States. These representatives, Webster and Hayne, were fitly chosen for the parts they had to perform; and, when the champion of chivalry assailed with extraordinary virulence and ability the character and institutions of Massachusetts and New England, he was met and overthrown by their defender in a strain of eloquence that no orator in this country has ever surpassed.

In 1858 these two States were

again in conflict on the same theatre and the same question in the persons of Wilson and Hammond; and we are constrained to say, without any hesitation, that Wilson's defence of Massachusetts is every way admirable, and worthy of a place by the side of the renowned effort of Daniel Webster. He does not, it is true, rest the case on the glories of Concord, Lexington, and Bunker Hill, or attempt to repaint the magnificent work of his great predecessor; but he is as just, as fervid, and as glowing, in setting forth the other and greater achievements of the people in the advancement of the arts and the principles of civilization. Is there any thing much better than this? —

"But the senator from South Carolina, after crowning Cotton as king, with power to bring England and all the civilized world 'toppling' down into the yawning gulfs of bankruptcy and ruin, complacently tells the Senate and the trembling subjects of his cotton-king that 'the greatest strength of the South arises from the harmony of her political and social institutions;' that 'her forms of society are the best in the world:' that 'she has an extent of political freedom, combined with entire security, seen nowhere on earth.' The South, he tells us, 'is satisfied, harmonious, and prosperous:' and he asks us if we have 'heard that the ghosts of Mendoza and Torquemada are stalking in the streets of our great cities; that the Inquisition is at hand; and that there are fearful rumors of consultations for vigilance committees.'

"Sir, this self-complacency is sublime. No son of the Celestial Empire can approach the senator in self-complacency. That 'society the best in the world' where more than three millions of beings created in the image of God are held as chattels, — sunk from the lofty level of humanity down to the abject condition of unreasoning beasts of burden! That 'society the best in the world' where are manacles, chains, and whips, auction-blocks, prisons, blood-hounds, scourgings, lynchings, and burnings; laws to torture the body, shrivel the mind, and debase the soul; where labor is dishonored, and the laborer despised! 'Political freedom' in a land where woman is imprisoned for teaching little children to read God's holy Word; where professors are deposed and banished for opposing the extension of slavery; where public men are exiled for quoting in a national convention the language of Jefferson; where voters are mobbed for appearing to vote for free territory; and where booksellers are driven from the country for selling that masterly work of genius, 'Uncle Tom's Cabin'! A land of 'certain security,' where patrols, costing, as in Old Virginia, more than is expended to educate her poor children, stalk the country to catch the faintest murmur of discontent; where the bay of the blood-hound never ceases; where, but little more than a year ago, there rose the startling cry of insurrection! 'Political freedom' and 'certain security' in a land which demands that seventeen millions of freemen shall stand guard to seize and carry back fleeing bondmen!"

Or is there any thing of the kind finer than this? —

"Mr. President, the senator from South Carolina tells us that 'all the powers of the world cannot abolish the thing' he calls slavery: 'God only can do it when he repeals the fiat, "The poor ye have always with you;" for the man who lives by daily labor, and your whole class of hireling manual laborers and operatives, are essentially slaves. Our slaves are black, happy, content, unaspiring: yours are white, and they feel galled by their degradation. Our slaves do not vote: yours do vote; and, being the majority, they are the depositaries of all your political power; and if they knew the tremendous secret, that the ballot-box is stronger than an army with banners, and could combine, your society would be reconstructed, your government overthrown, and your property divided.'

"'The poor ye have always with you.' This fiat of Almighty God, which Christian men of all ages and lands have accepted as the imperative injunction of the common Father of all to care for the children of misfortune and sorrow, the senator from South Carolina accepts as the foundation-stone, the eternal law, of slavery, which 'all the powers of earth cannot abolish.' These precious words of our heavenly Father, 'the poor ye have always with you,' are perpetually sounding in the ears of mankind, ever reminding them of their dependence and their duties. These words appeal alike to the conscience and the heart of mankind. To men blessed in their basket and their store they say, 'Property has its duties as well as its rights.' To men clothed with authority to shape the policy or to administer the laws of the State they say, 'Lighten, by wise, humane, and equal laws, the burdens of the toiling and dependent children of men.' To men of every age and every clime they appeal by the divine promise, that 'he that giveth to the poor lendeth to the Lord.' Sir, I thank God that I live in a Commonwealth which sees no warrant in these words of inspiration to oppress the sons and daughters of toil and poverty. Over the poor and lowly she casts the broad shield of equal, just, and humane legislation. The poorest man that treads her soil, no matter what blood may run in his veins, is protected in his rights, and incited to labor, by no other force than the assurance that the fruits of his toil belong to himself, to the wife of his bosom, and the children of his love.

"The senator from South Carolina exclaims, 'The man who lives by daily labor, your whole class of manual laborers, are essentially slaves: they feel galled by their degradation.' What a sentiment is this to hear uttered in the councils of this democratic republic! The senator's political associates who listen to these words, which brand hundreds of thousands of the men they represent in the free States, and hundreds of their neighbors and personal friends, as 'slaves,' have found no words to repel or rebuke this language. This language of scorn and contempt is addressed to senators who were not nursed by a slave; whose lot it was to toil with their own hands; to eat bread earned, not by the sweat of another's brow, but by their own. Sir, I am the son of a 'hireling manual laborer,' who, with the frosts of seventy winters on his brow, 'lives by daily labor.' I, too, have been a 'hireling manual laborer.' Poverty cast its dark and chilling shadow over the home of my childhood; and Want was there sometimes, an unbidden guest. At the age of ten years, to aid him who gave me being in keeping the gaunt spectre from the hearth of the mother who bore me, I left the home of my boyhood, and went to earn my bread by 'daily labor.' Many a weary mile have I travelled

'To beg a brother of the earth
To give me leave to toil.'

"Sir, I have toiled as a 'hireling manual laborer' in the field and in the workshop: and I tell the senator from South Carolina that I never 'felt galled by my degradation.' No, sir; never! Perhaps the senator who represents that 'other class, which leads progress, civilization, and refinement,' will ascribe this to obtuseness of intellect and blunted sensibilities of the heart. Sir, I was conscious of my manhood: I was the peer of my employer. I knew that the laws and institutions of my native and adopted States threw over him and over me alike the panoply of equality: I knew, too, that the world was before me; that its wealth, its garnered treasures of knowledge, its honors, the coveted prizes of life, were within the grasp of a brave heart and a tireless hand; and I accepted the responsibilities of my position, all unconscious that I was a 'slave.' I have employed others, — hundreds of 'hireling manual laborers.' Some of them possessed, and now possess, more property than I ever owned; some of them were better educated than myself; yes, sir, better educated, and better read too, than some senators on this floor; and many of them, in moral excellence and purity of character, I could not but feel, were my superiors. I have occupied, Mr. President, for more than thirty years, the relation of employer and employed; and, while I never felt 'galled by my degradation' in the one case, in the other I was never conscious that my 'hireling laborers' were my inferiors. That man is a 'snob' who boasts of being a 'hireling laborer,' or who is ashamed of being a 'hireling laborer;' that man is a 'snob' who feels any inferiority to any man because he is a 'hireling laborer,' or who assumes any superiority over others because he is an employer. Honest labor is honorable; and the man who is ashamed that he is or was a 'hireling laborer' has not manhood enough to 'feel galled by his degradation.'

"Having occupied, Mr. President, the relation of either employed or employer for a third of a century, having lived in a Commonwealth where the 'hireling class of manual laborers' are 'the depositaries of political power,' having associated with this class in all the relations of life, I tell the senator from South Carolina, and the class he represents, that he libels, grossly libels them, when he declares that they are 'essentially slaves.' There can be found nowhere in America a class of men more proudly conscious or tenacious of their rights. Friends and foes have ever found them

'A stubborn race, fearing and flattering none.'

"Ours are the institutions of freedom; and they flourish best in the storms and agitations of inquiry and free discussion. We are conscious that our social and political institutions have not attained perfection; and we invoke the examination and criticism of all the genius and learning of all Christendom. Should the senator and his agitators and lecturers come to Massachusetts on a mission to teach our 'hireling class of manual laborers,' our 'mud-sills,' our 'slaves,' the 'tremendous secret of the ballot-box,' and to help 'combine and lead them,' these stigmatized 'hirelings' would reply to the senator and his associates, 'We are freemen; we are the peers of the gifted and the wealthy; we know the "tremendous secret of the ballot-box;" and we mould and fashion these institutions that bless and adorn our proud and free Commonwealth. These public schools are ours, for the education of our children; these libraries, with their accumulated treasures, are ours; these multitudinous and varied pursuits of life, where intelligence and skill find their reward, are ours. Labor is here honored and respected, and great examples incite us to action. All around us, in the professions, in the marts of commerce, on the exchange, where merchant-princes and capitalists do congregate; in these manufactories and workshops, where the products of every clime are fashioned into a thousand forms of utility and beauty; on these smiling farms, fertilized by the sweat of free labor, — in every position of private and of public life are our associates, who were but yesterday "hireling laborers," "mud-sills," "slaves." In every department of human effort are noble men who sprang from our ranks, — men whose good deeds will be felt, and will live in the grateful memories of men, when the stones reared by the hands of affection to their honored names shall crumble into dust. Our eyes glisten and our hearts throb over the bright, glowing, and radiant pages of our history, that record the deeds of patriotism of the sons of New England, who sprang from our ranks, and wore the badges of toil. While the names of Benjamin Franklin, Roger Sherman, Nathaniel Greene, and Paul Revere, live on the brightest pages of our history, the mechanics of Massachusetts and New England will never want illustrious examples to incite them to noble aspirations and noble deeds. Go home: say to your privileged class, which, you vauntingly say, "leads progress, civilization, and refinement," that it is the opinion of the "hireling laborers" of Massachusetts, if you have no sympathy for your African bondmen, in whose veins flows so much of your own blood, you should at least sympathize with the millions of your own race, whose labor you have dishonored and degraded by slavery. You should teach your millions of poor and ignorant white men, so long oppressed by your policy, the "tremendous secret, that the ballot-box is stronger than an army with banners." You should combine, and lead them to the adoption of a policy which shall secure their own emancipation from a degrading thraldom.'"

This speech of Wilson's is one of the best ever made in the Senate. It astonished the friends of the "peculiar institution," and confounded their "self-complacency," in a way, and to such a degree, that they never recovered it.

CHAPTER XII.

The Crittenden Compromise.

THE Crittenden Compromise is seldom mentioned in these days, because it failed, and therefore was never able to do any mischief. Had it passed, it might have prolonged the agitations and evils of the period for a time, and postponed the war to a future day; when, instead of Abraham Lincoln or U. S. Grant to deal with, the disunionists might encounter some later Buchanan, or other person in favor of letting the "wayward sisters" go; and then rebellion must have succeeded. Mr. Crittenden was a disciple and follower of Henry Clay, and, of course, a believer in compromises for the cure of the diseases of the body politic. He was an able man, and honest and patriotic: but to argue that because Mr. Clay once saved the Union by a compromise, therefore that was a sure and proper remedy, was not the perfection of human reason: but it was as far as Mr. Crittenden had gone.

The compromises of Mr. Clay had been very prolific, and fearfully bad breeders. When the spoiled children and "wayward sisters" found they could gain their points by threats, they threatened and increased their demands; and, when this was done, there were plenty of statesmen desirous of imitating the brilliant success of Mr. Clay, and, to save the Union, would give away every thing that made the Union worth having. Mr. Crittenden was not probably conscious of the extent to which his scheme went in this direction, and acted with a sincere desire to heal our difficulties; but Wilson fitly characterized it as a surrender. The resolutions were offered by Crittenden Dec. 18, 1860, and elicited a debate of remarkable interest and ability. Wilson felt the momentous importance of the crisis, and prepared himself to meet it in a manner worthy of a representative of the old State of Massachusetts, worthy of an American senator, worthy of a citizen of the great republic; and he did thus meet it. On the evening of 21st February he obtained leave to speak out of order, and addressed the full Senate, and an audience in the galleries, which were packed to their full capacity. Mr. Victor, in his able history of the Rebellion, says the speech was one of the most elaborate of the session. "As an argument it was masterly. As a statement it was more than individual in its opinions: it echoed the predominant sentiment of the unconditional unionists of the North." It was, in fact, one of the ablest, most eloquent, and thrilling speeches ever made in Congress; and, had Wilson never made but this one, it would have been sufficient to have given him a national reputation.

It is impossible to quote the whole, and not easy to give a portion without injuring the effect; but we transcribe a passage or two:—

"The senator from Texas (Mr. Wigfall) graciously assures us of the North, that if we will suppress our pulpits and schools and presses, which teach our people that slavery is a wrong, and recognize the rightfulness of property in the bodies and souls of men, then they will condescend to take into consideration the question of continuing in the Union. The senator dreams of Northern campaigns,—of going into winter-quarters at the Continental Hotel in Philadelphia, the Fifth-avenue House in New York, and the Revere House in Boston. He talks of dictating a treaty of peace in Faneuil Hall, on Plymouth Rock, or at Bunker Hill. That senator evidently has little faith in the capacities of the North for a contest of arms, should it come upon us; while he magnifies the power of the South. Sons who bear the names and inherit the blood of an ancestry that rose at the sound of the alarm-gun on the morn of the Revolution, and followed the flag of independence over stricken fields to the crowning glories of Yorktown, who crossed bayonets with British veterans on the bloody heights of Lundy's Lane, and covered your youthful navy with renown on ocean and on lake, are not 'less valiant than the virgin in the night, and skilless as unpractised infancy.' We freely concede the bravery of our countrymen of the South, and we do so in spite of their gasconade and boastful vauntings of chivalric courage. We of the North are quite confident we are as strong of arm, as skilled of hand, and as fleet of foot, as are our more boastful countrymen of the sunny South; that we can endure toil and cold and hunger as well as they; and I am sure the senator from Texas will admit we can endure thirst quite as well as they.

"But the senator from Texas tells us that money is the sinew of war; that we of the North have no money; that they gather gold in hundreds of millions from the stalk of the cotton-plant. They send the negro, he says, to the field: he gathers cotton from the stalk, brings it to the gin-house, puts it through the necessary process, and rolls out a bale of five ten-dollar gold-pieces. But the senator did not tell us that it might have cost six ten-dollar gold-pieces to get this bale of five ten-dollar gold-pieces. The senator seems to belong to that class of political economists that never count the cost of maintaining 'King Cotton.' I would remind the senator that we of the North take this bale of cotton the negro picks, pay the five ten-dollar gold-pieces, stamp upon it our skill, art, civilization; send it back; and they of the South promise to give five bales of the next crop for it: but I regret to say, sir, we are often forced to take fewer than are promised. I would remind the boastful senator that the people of the cotton confederacy are in debt to the amount of millions; that they are not paying fifty cents on the dollar of their indebtedness; that the proceeds of the last cotton-crop will not extinguish that indebtedness. I would remind the senator — who tells us we of the North have no money, that they pick it by millions from the stalk of the cotton-plant — that the working-men of Massachusetts, whom gentlemen of the South predicted would be in a state of starvation and insurrection ere this, have on deposit in the savings-banks alone forty-five millions of dollars, — millions more than are deposited in all the banks of the seven seceding States by merchants, bankers, planters, and all classes of their people.

"The senator from Illinois (Mr. Douglas) ostentatiously assumes to rise above parties and creeds and platforms, up to the level of the occasion. I commend his avowed purpose; but I am constrained to say, after listening to his speeches, that he has hardly come up to the promised position. Underneath all his vaunting professions of readiness to ignore party creeds and platforms, and to know nothing but the Union, the senator discloses his eagerness to join in the reconstruction of the broken ranks of the Democracy, and his readiness to avail himself of passing events to achieve the desired object. To that end he is evidently quite ready, perhaps quite anxious, to surrender his 'great principle:' he cannot, therefore, fully appreciate the motives and action of those who are less facile than himself.

"The senator from Illinois brings against us of the Republican party the accusation, that, after having brought the country to the verge of destruction, we will not accept the compromise measures of the senator from Kentucky (Mr. Crittenden); and are therefore, notwithstanding our professions, not devoted to the perpetuity of the Union. Sir, I do not understand what the senator means by these accusations against us of having brought the country to the verge of destruction, and of not being faithful to the Union. We did not at Charleston or Baltimore plot the disruption of the Democratic party as the first step to disunion, nor secretly plot the dismemberment of the confederacy, or the seizure of the government; we have not been in complicity with secessionists, chaffering for the postponement of rebellion until after the 4th of March; nor have we sat in councils of the executive, conspiring with plotters of rebellions, ruining the credit of the country, converting the war-office into an organization for robbing the public treasury, swindling the people, and betraying the country — its forts, arms, arsenals, ships — into the hands of disloyal men. No, sir; no! We have violated no law, human or divine; performed no acts not sanctioned by law, humanity, and religion.

"Whatever may be the issue of this wicked, causeless revolt against the government, we are ready to abide the judgment of liberty-loving, law-abiding men of the present and of coming ages.

"The venerable senator from Kentucky (Mr. Crittenden) comes forward with his plan of adjustment: he stands forth as a pacificator, commissioned to compromise and adjust pending issues to give repose to the distracted country. I most cheerfully accord to the senator from Kentucky purity of motive, and patriotic intentions and purposes. While I believe every pulsation of his heart throbs for the unity and perpetuity of the republic, while I cherish for him sentiments of sincere respect and regard, I am constrained to say, here and now, that his policy has been most fatal to the repose of the country, if not to the integrity of the Union and the authority of the government. Whether his task be self-imposed, or whether it be imposed upon him by others, he has stood forth day by day, not to sustain the Constitution, the Union, and the enforcement of the laws, not to rebuke seditious words and treasonable acts, but to demand the incorporation into the organic law of the nation unrepealable, degrading, and humiliating concessions to the dark spirit of slavery. Had the acknowledged chiefs of secession, or their Northern confederates, put forth these demands for concessions to slavery, they would have been promptly and indignantly rejected by the people of the North. Put forth in the honored name of the venerable senator from Kentucky, they have received support enough to encourage the secessionists in their demands for concessions which can never, *no, never*, be made by the freemen of the North. The almost certain rejection of these propositions by the North the secessionists are using to deceive the people of the South concerning the sentiments of the people of the free States, and to lead them into secession and disunion. The ancient philosopher thought he could move the world if he could find a fulcrum for his lever: the secessionists seem to act as if they had found a fulcrum for their disunion lever in the proposition of the senator from Kentucky, which, in bitter irony, is called a compromise. . . .

"The senator from Kentucky, seconded by the senator from Illinois, proposes to incorporate in the Constitution a provision that 'THE ELECTIVE FRANCHISE SHALL NOT BE EXERCISED BY ANY PERSONS OF THE AFRICAN RACE, IN WHOLE OR IN PART.' Why, sir, is this proposition of disfranchisement now made? Who demands it? What is to be gained by this disfranchisement of men whose ancestors possessed the right of suffrage before the Constitution of the United States came from the hands of its illustrious framers? . . .

"Massachusetts adopted her Constitution in 1780, during the war of independence. That Constitution made the slave a freeman; made persons of the African race citizens, entitled to the elective franchise. This right, secured in the troublous days of the Revolution to persons of the African race by John Adams, Parsons, Lowell, and their noble associates, has been exercised for eighty years. Now, sir, the senator from Kentucky comes into this chamber, and proposes the disfranchisement and degradation of citizens of Massachusetts, made so by her heroic sires; and I blush to confess that there are men in that Commonwealth so false and recreant to human rights as to petition Congress to sustain this wicked, this monstrous proposition of disfranchisement. I know, sir, it is an ungracious task, in these days and in these chambers, to maintain even the legal rights of a proscribed race. I am not insensible to the gibes and jeers, the taunts and misrepresentations, of a corrupted public opinion; but I never can, I never will, consent, by word or act, to this crime against freemen. The material interests of Massachusetts are dear to me; but the rights of her people are far dearer. Still I tell her apostate sons, who have put their names to these memorials for the disfranchisement of her colored men, knowing what they did, that the constitutional rights of the humblest man who treads the soil of the old Puritan Commonwealth are dearer, far dearer, to me, than all those material interests for which they are ready to sacrifice the rights of their fellow-men.

"Sir, in the dark days of our weakness, the ancestors of the men you would now, in the days of your power, trample beneath your feet, freely gave their blood for the liberties and independence of America. The leader and first victim of the Boston massacre of the 5th of March, 1770, which so fired the hearts and roused the patriotism of the people, was Crispus Attucks, a colored patriot. One of that race mingled his blood with the fallen patriots of the 19th of April, 1775; and they stood with our heroic sires on the heights of Bunker Hill when the storm of battle clung around and beat upon it. They fought side by side, and shoulder to shoulder, with our fathers; 'for the right,' says Bancroft in his narration of the work of that day, 'of the free negroes to bear arms in the public defence at that day was as little disputed in New England as their other rights.' When Major Pitcairn — the leader who opened the murderous fire upon the patriots on the green of Lexington Common — mounted the works on Bunker Hill, crying, 'The day is ours!' he fell mortally wounded by the unerring shot of Salem, a black soldier.

"Hundreds of the ancestors of the men upon whose brows the senator from Kentucky would stamp degradation entered the army, and fought with heroic courage on the stricken fields of the Revolution. Some of the most heroic deeds of the war of independence were performed by black men. A braver regiment than the colored regiment of Rhode Island, led by the gallant Col. Greene, the hero of Red Bank, trod not the battle-fields of the Revolution. Of this black regiment Tristam Burges said in the House of Representatives, in 1828, that 'no braver men met the enemy in battle;' and Gov. Eustis of Massachusetts, secretary of war under Jefferson, said of them in 1820, 'They discharged their duty with zeal and fidelity. The gallant defence of Red Bank, in which the black regiment bore a part, is among the proofs of their valor.' Arnold, in his admirable History of Rhode Island, pays this noble tribute to the conduct of a regiment in the battle of Rhode Island, which Lafayette pronounced 'the best-fought battle of the war:' 'It was in repelling these furious onsets that the newly-raised *black regiment*, under Col. Greene, distinguished itself by deeds of desperate valor. Posted behind a thicket in the valley, they three times drove back the Hessians, who repeatedly charged down the hill to dislodge them; and so determined were the enemy in these successive charges, that, the day after the battle, the Hessian colonel upon whom this duty had devolved applied to exchange his command, and go to New York, because he dared not lead his regiment again to battle, lest his men should shoot him for having caused them so much loss.'

"Connecticut, too, raised a battalion of black soldiers; and Col. Humphrey, attached to the military family of Washington, accepted a command in this corps. The heroic defence of the fort on the heights of Groton by Col. Ledyard and his brave comrades is a glorious page in our history. By their side fought and fell men of this hated race. History records, that, when the works were stormed, the British officer, exasperated by the heroic resistance, inquired, 'Who commands this fort?' —'I once did; you do now,' answered Ledyard, handing the officer his sword, which was instantly run through his body by the officer. Lambert, a black soldier, avenged this murder of his commander by thrusting his bayonet through the body of the British officer, and then fell pierced by thirty-three bayonet-wounds. Sir, in the great struggle for independence, in the war of 1812, on land and sea, the blood of the colored men of New England was freely poured out in vindication of your liberties, rights, and honor; and now you ask us to despoil them of their long-possessed rights. Never, sir, never, by my consent! In addressing the German working-men of Cincinnati the other day, Mr. Lincoln told them that 'they were all of the great family of men; and, if there is one shackle upon any of them, it would be far better to lift the load from them than to pile additional loads upon them.' That was the utterance of a Christian statesman. These men you propose to disfranchise forever are all of the great family of men; and, if there are shackles upon them, it would be far better to lift the load from them than to pile additional burdens upon them."

CHAPTER XIII.

The People of Color. — What Wilson has done for Them.

WHAT Henry Wilson has attempted and accomplished for the colored race is not likely to be forgotten by them; but it is due to history that it be stated in a concise form in this volume.

On the 4th of December, 1861, after the announcement of the standing committees of the Senate, Mr. Wilson of Massachusetts introduced a resolution, that all laws in force relating to the arrest of fugitives from service, and all laws concerning persons of color, within the District, be referred to the Committee on the District of Columbia; and that the committee be instructed to consider the expediency of abolishing slavery in the District, with compensation to loyal holders of slaves. Mr. Grimes of Iowa was chairman of this committee. In moving the reference of his resolution to this committee, Mr. Wilson expressed the hope that the chairman "would deal promptly with the question."

On the 16th of December Mr.

Wilson introduced a bill for the release of certain persons held to service or labor in the District of Columbia. The bill provided for the immediate emancipation of the slaves, for the payment to their loyal owners of an average sum of three hundred dollars, for the appointment of a commission to assess the sum to be paid, and the appropriation of a million of dollars.

Mr. Wilson, on the 24th of February, introduced a bill to repeal certain laws and ordinances in the District of Columbia relating to persons of color, and moved its reference to the District Committee. This bill proposed to repeal the acts of Congress extending over the District of Columbia relating to persons of color, to annul and abrogate those laws, to repeal the acts giving the cities of Washington and Georgetown authority to pass ordinances relating to persons of color, to abrogate those ordinances, and to make persons of color amenable to the same laws to which free white persons are amenable, and to subject them to the same penalties and punishments.

On the 25th Mr. Wilson addressed the Senate in favor of the bill he had introduced early in the session.

"This bill, to give liberty to the bondman," he said, "deals justly, ay, generously, by the master. The American people, whose moral sense has been outraged by slavery and the black codes enacted in the interests of slavery in the District of Columbia, whose fame has been soiled and dimmed by the deeds of cruelty perpetrated in their national capital, would stand justified in the forum of nations if they should smite the fetter from the bondman, regardless of the desires or interests of the master. With generous magnanimity, this bill tenders compensation to the master out of the earnings of the toiling freemen of America. . . . In what age of the world, in what land under the whole heavens, can you find any enactment of equal atrocity to this iniquitous and profligate statute, this 'legal presumption' that color is evidence that man, made in the image of God, is an 'absconding slave'? This monstrous doctrine, abhorrent to every manly impulse of the heart, to every Christian sentiment of the soul, to every deduction of human reason, which the refined, humane, and Christian people of America have upheld for two generations, which the corporation of Washington enacted into an imperative ordinance, has borne its legitimate fruits of injustice and inhumanity, of dishonor and shame. Crimes against man, in the name of this abhorred doctrine, have been annually perpetrated in this national capital, which should make the people of America hang their heads in shame before the nations, and in abasement before that Being who keeps watch and ward over the humblest of the children of men. . . . Here the oath of the black man affords no protection whatever to his property, to the fruits of his toil, to the personal rights of himself, his wife, his children, or his race. Greedy avarice may withhold from him the fruits of his toil, or clutch from him his little acquisitions; the brutal may visit upon him, his wife, his children, insults, indignities, blows; the kidnapper may enter his dwelling, and steal from his hearthstone his loved ones; the assassin may hover on his track, imperilling his household; every outrage that the depravity of man can visit upon his brother-man may be perpetrated upon him, upon his family, his race: but his oath upon the evangelists of Almighty God, though his name may be written in the book of life, neither protects him from wrong, nor punishes the wrong-doer. This Christian nation, in solemn mockery, enacts that the free black men of America shall not bear testimony in the judicial tribunals of the District of Columbia. Although the black man is thus mute and dumb before the judicial tribunals of the capital of Christian America, his wrongs we have not righted here will go up to a higher tribunal, where the oath of the proscribed negro is heard, and his story registered by the pen of the recording angel. . . . These colonial statutes of Maryland, re-affirmed by Congress in 1801, these ordinances of Washington and Georgetown, sanctioned in advance by the authority of the Federal Government, stand this day unrepealed. Such laws and ordinances should not be permitted longer to insult the reason, pervert the moral sense, or offend the taste, of the people of America. Any people mindful of the decencies of life would not longer permit such enactments to linger before the eye of civilized man. Slavery is the prolific mother of those monstrous enactments. Bid slavery disappear from the District of Columbia, and it will take along with it this whole brood of brutal, vulgar, and indecent statutes. . . . This bill for the release of persons held to services or labor in the District of Columbia, and the compensation of loyal masters from the treasury of the United States, was prepared after much reflection, and some consultation with others. The committee on the District of Columbia in both Houses, to whom it was referred, have agreed to it, with a few amendments calculated to carry out more completely its original purposes and provisions. I trust that the bill as it now stands, after the adoption of the amendments proposed by the senator from Maine (Mr. Morrill), will speedily pass without any material modifications. If it shall become the law of the land, it will blot out slavery forever from the national capital, transform three thousand personal chattels into freemen, obliterate oppressive, odious, and hateful laws and ordinances which press with merciless force upon persons, bond or free, of African descent, and relieve the nation from the responsibilities now pressing upon it. An act of beneficence like this will be hailed and applauded by the nations, sanctified by justice, humanity, and religion, by the approving voice of conscience, and by the blessing of Him who bids us 'break every yoke, undo the heavy burden, and let the oppressed go free.'"

After considerable discussion, this bill, introduced by Mr. Wilson into the Senate Dec. 16, 1861, passed the Senate April 3, 1862, by a vote of twenty-nine to fourteen.

On the 1st of May, 1862, Mr.

Wilson moved to substitute for the sixth section of Mr. Collamer's amendment to a bill introduced by Mr. Trumbull in December, 1861, which provided for the freeing of the slaves of rebels. "That, in any State in which the inhabitants have by the president been heretofore declared in a state of insurrection, the president is required, for the speedy and more effectual suppression of said insurrection, within thirty days after the passage of this act, to appoint a day when all persons holden to service in any such State (whose service is by the law of said State due to one who, after the passage of this act, shall levy war or participate in insurrection against the United States, or give aid to the same) shall be forever free, any law to the contrary nothwithstanding." In support of this amendment, Mr. Wilson said, —

"I am free to confess that the provision emancipating the slaves of rebels is, with me, the chief object of solicitude. I do not expect that we shall realize any large amount of property by any confiscation bill that we shall pass. After the conflict, when the din of battle has ceased, the humane and kindly and charitable feelings of the country and of the world will require us to deal gently with the masses of the people who are engaged in this rebellion. It will be pleaded that wives and children will suffer for the crimes of husbands and fathers; and such appeals will have more or less effect upon the future policy of the government. But, sir, take from your rebel masters their bondmen, and from the hour you do so until the end of the world, to 'the last syllable of recorded time,' the judgment of the country and the judgment of the world will sanction the act. . . . Slavery is the great rebel, the giant criminal, the murderer striving with bloody hands to throttle our government and destroy our country. Senators may talk round it, if they please; they may scold at its agents, and denounce its tools: I care little about its agents or its tools. I think not of Davis and his compeers in crime: I look at the thing itself, — to the great rebel with hands dripping with the blood of my murdered countrymen. I give the criminal no quarter. If I, with the light I have, could utter a word or give a vote to continue for one moment the life of the great rebel that is now striking at the vitals of my country, I should feel that I was a traitor to my native land, and deserved a traitor's doom. . . . While I would not take the lives of many, if any; while I would not take the property of more than the leaders, — I would take the bondman from every rebel on the continent; and, in doing it, I should have the sanction of my own judgment, the sanction of the enlightened world, the sanction of the coming ages, and the blessing of Almighty God. Every day while the world stands, the act will be approved and applauded by the human heart all over the globe. . . . When slavery is stricken down, they will come back again, and offer their hands, red though they be with the blood of our brethren; and we shall forgive the past, take them to our bosoms, and be again one people. But, senators, keep slavery; let it stand; shrink from duty; let men whose hands are stained with the blood of our countrymen, whose hearts are disloyal to our country, hold fast to the chains that bind three millions of men in bondage, — and we shall have an enemy to hate us, ready to seize on all fit opportunities to smite down all that we love, and again to raise their disloyal hands against the perpetuity of the republic. Sir, I believe this to be as true as the holy evangelists of Almighty God; and nothing but the prejudices of association on the one side, or timidity on the other, can hold us back from doing the duty we owe to our country in this crisis."

On the 6th of May Mr. Wilson withdrew his amendment to Mr. Collamer's substitute for the original bill, but offered another amendment as a substitute for Mr. Collamer's substitute for the original bill. Mr. Wilson said, "He (Mr. Collamer) puts it in the discretion of the president. My amendment makes it imperative upon the president to issue his proclamation, immediately after the passage of the act, to fix a day, not more than thirty days after the act is passed, when the slaves of all persons who engage in insurrection or rebellion after they have had the warning of thirty days after the time is fixed, shall be made free." Again he says, "I feel deeply upon this question. The conviction is upon me that this is the path of duty to my country, and that the future peace of the nation requires that this slave interest shall be broken down; and now is the opportunity, — an opportunity that only comes to nations once in ages. It comes to us now. Let us hail and improve it." After various amendments the bill passed, leaving it discretionary with the president when to issue the proclamation.

On the 29th of April, 1862, Mr. Wilson moved to amend a bill providing for the education of colored youth in the District of Columbia, introduced by Mr. Grimes of Iowa, by adding as an additional section, —

"That all persons of color in the District of Columbia, or in the corporate limits of the cities of Washington and Georgetown, shall be subject and amenable to the same laws and ordinances to which free white persons are or may be subject or amenable; that they shall be tried for any offences against the laws in the same manner as free white persons are or may be tried for the same offences; and that, upon being legally convicted of any crime or offence against any law or ordinance, such persons of color shall be liable to the same penalty or punishment, and no other, as would be imposed or inflicted upon free white persons for the same crime or offence; and all acts, or parts of acts, inconsistent with the provisions of this act, are hereby repealed."

Let us now recapitulate the important measures set on foot by Senator Wilson in this behalf: —

1. He introduced the bill to abol-

ish slavery in the District of Columbia. Dec. 16, 1861, by which three thousand were made free, and all slavery in the District was made illegal in the future.

2. A bill that persons of color in the District should be treated in law the same as white persons. This bill became a law 21 May, 1862.

3. A bill to amend the act of 1795 concerning the militia, by which the colored men could be enlisted as soldiers. and all slaves made soldiers; their wives and children to be free if they were slaves of persons in rebellion. This bill became a law July 17, 1862. In the committee of conference on the House Enrolment Bill, Mr. Wilson moved that drafted slaves should be made free on entering the service; and the motion prevailed. Gen. Palmer of Illinois reported, that, in Kentucky, twenty thousand were made free by this provision.

4. A bill making the wives and children of drafted men free; and this, according to the report of Gen. Palmer, liberated seventy thousand women and children in the State of Kentucky. The number made free in other border States is unknown, but must have been very great. A writer estimates the whole number of persons made free under the above-named measures at two hundred and fifty thousand.

5. He moved a section as an amendment to the Appropriation Bill of 1864, to give colored soldiers the same perquisites and pay as white soldiers.

6. He was chairman of the Committee of Conference on the Freedman's Bureau, and reported the measure.

7. A motion by which land purchased by government at tax-sales in South Carolina should be offered to freedmen in lots of forty acres at a nominal price to enable them to obtain homesteads.

8. A bill to abolish peonage in New Mexico, to strike the word "white" from the militia-laws, and to prohibit punishment of offences by whipping.

9. A bill to incorporate the Freedmen's Savings Bank.

10. A bill to incorporate Howard University.

11. A joint resolution, March 7, 1862, to aid Maryland and Delaware to abolish slavery.

12. A bill, May 24, 1862, to give colored persons claimed as fugitives from servitude the right of trial by jury.

On all these various important measures Mr. Wilson spoke with earnestness, and a logic that was unanswerable. He worked early and late to get them in shape to secure their passage. They were passed, and are to-day almost unanimously approved by the people of the country. Surely no monument could add to the honor of a man whose skill and devotion have secured so much to the benefit of the slave, so much to the glory of the country.

When, in consequence largely of the efforts of Senator Wilson, the colored race were able to avail themselves of the right of equality before the law, and sent to the United-States Senate one of their own number in the person of H. R. Revels of Mississippi, it was Henry Wilson who had the satisfaction of being selected to present his credentials, and thus practically to announce, that, in national councils, caste had been abolished.

CHAPTER XIV.

Military. — As Chairman of Senate Committee on Military Affairs.

PRACTICALLY Mr. Wilson succeeded Jeff. Davis as chairman of the Military Committee of the Senate, little military business having been done after Davis left. As Mr. Stanton received the merited appellation of "the great war secretary" of Mr. Lincoln's administration, there seems little less pertinence in styling Mr. Wilson the "war senator" during the same momentous period. It is doing injustice to no other member of Congress to say that no one else of either House was more active, untiring, and influential, than was the junior senator of Massachusetts. Not only as chairman of the Committee on Military Affairs was he officially connected with the military legislation of Congress during those terrible years, but the report of its proceedings reveals the fact that he introduced, managed, debated, and carried through the Senate, more important measures than any other member. The same report also shows that he was not only found advocating those advanced ideas of human equality and justice which had marked his previous political history, but that he brought to the task of legislating for the new order of things his usual practical sagacity, and sense of equity, which prompted him, while doing justice to all, to do injustice to none.

Immediately after the beginning of hostilities, the president issued his proclamation for an extra session of Congress. Assembling according to such invitation, it met at noon on the 4th of July, 1861. On the same day, Mr. Wilson gave notice of his intention to introduce into the Senate the following four bills and one joint resolution: —

A bill to authorize the employment of volunteers to aid in enforcing the laws, &c.

A bill to increase the military establishment of the United States.

A bill providing for the better organization of the military establishment.

A bill for the organization of a volunteer militia force, &c.; and

A joint resolution to ratify and confirm certain acts of the president for the suppression of insurrection and rebellion.

According to the notice given, he introduced these several bills on the 6th to the consideration of the two Houses and the country, and entered at once and vigorously upon the task of preparing and persuading the minds of both for their adoption.

The bill for the employment of volunteers encountered differences of opinion. especially on two points, — the number of troops to be called out. and the mode of securing their officering. In the original bill the president was authorized to "accept such numbers as he might deem necessary." An amendment was proposed, substituting for these words "five hundred thousand men." Mr. Saulsbury of Delaware, expressing his fears that "the Union could not be preserved by the mode contemplated in this bill," moved to substitute for "five hundred thousand men" "two hundred thousand men;" which Mr. Foster of Connecticut intimated were "too many to make peace, and too few to make war." Mr. Wilson moved as an amendment, that "the president be authorized to accept the services of volunteers in such numbers, not exceeding five hundred thousand men, as he may deem necessary for the purpose" proposed, "equalizing as far as practicable the number furnished by the several States."

On the second point, that of providing officers for the new troops, there arose at once questions not without their difficulties, on which it was all but inevitable that there should be discrepant opinions and antagonistic claims. To do justice to the regular army, and at the same time to allow the army to do no injustice to the country, to appreciate and appropriate for the new service whatever of good the former contained, and at the same time, and for the same reason, not to imperil the latter by giving commands to epauletted incompetence while withholding them from men in civil life who had both the necessary talent and tact, was not an easy task; and yet that was the course Mr. Wilson sought to pursue, the policy he attempted to adopt. Upon a motion that the president might select major-generals and brigadier-generals for the regular army, he said, "There are several officers in the army. of great distinction, who would make excellent major and brigadier generals. I think, and have thought, that those men ought to be selected in preference to civilians, however eminent they may be in talent and character." Though these were his sentiments, he afterwards offered an amendment, which was accepted, that the "governors of States furnishing volunteers under this act shall commission the field, staff, and company officers requisite for the said volunteers."

Upon the bill to increase the regular army, a motion was made that no persons should be made major or brigadier generals who had not served ten years, and no person should be colonel, lieutenant-colonel, or major, who had not served two years, in the regular army. Mr. Wilson opposed the restriction. While his action on the previous bill had revealed his purpose to stand by the regular army, do justice to its members, and regard with respectful deference all proper "regulations," it was equally plain that there were considerations paramount even to them. They were the safety of the beleaguered government and of the imperilled nation. There was something more sacred in his eyes than "red tape" and "seniority" in the army. Accordingly, after alluding to the fact that "one-half of the officers should be taken from the old army," he pleaded for the policy that would draw largely from the recognized abilities and patriotism that shone and burned in the civil walks of life. "Thousands of the young men of the country," he said, "from law-schools and colleges, are applying for commissions; and the government can select young men of talent and character. There never was a time in the history of the country when men of talent, men of culture, men of experience, men of fortune, were seeking as they are now seeking admission into the army." Alluding to some irregularity that had been complained of, he said, "The object is to get a military force into the field as soon as possible; and the government is of course compelled by the exigencies of the service, by the condition of the country, to do in this case what it has been compelled to do in some other cases, — disregard forms and regulations." The object had been, he said, "in departing from the rule of seniority in the appointments, to take officers who were fitted for responsible positions to make the army most effective."

Objections having been urged against some features of the bill because of the danger of entailing upon the country a gigantic debt and a "standing army," which, said Mr. Nesmith of Oregon, "no man here will live to see smaller," Mr. Wilson expressed his willingness to leave that matter to the future. "This country understands," he said, "its own interests: and, when this contest is closed, the public burdens will be such that the people will seek all proper ways to reduce their expenditures; and, if there is a man in the army more than they want, they will strike that man's name from the rolls. Believing that the people then will know what they want, what their own interests require, and that they will be just as competent to decide this question as we are to-day, I choose to leave the question with them."

To the bill for the better organization of the military establishment, which, as reported on the 6th, contained eighteen sections, Mr. Wilson, on the 17th, offered an amendment, in the form of a substitute, containing twenty sections. In explanation of its provisions he said, "I have labored night and day for many days and nights to fit and prepare this bill to meet the actual wants of the country; and, in doing so, I have had to meet the interests, the jealousies, or the prejudices, of men connected with the army of the United States: but, in framing it, I have endeavored to be governed wholly by the public interest, and not by the wants and wishes of any particular men in the army or in the departments."

The joint resolution to approve and confirm certain acts of the president for suppressing insurrection and rebellion of course excited much opposition, and led to acrimonious debate. In the course of the debate, the action of the government in Maryland had been pronounced by one of its senators as "positive, arbitrary, causeless, and wanton oppression;" while another had asked Mr. Wilson if he was "apprised of any necessity for the suspension of the writ of *habeas corpus* in that State."

He replied affirmatively, expressing the conviction that a city which harbored and encouraged the conspirators who fired on the Massachusetts troops, as, obedient to their country's call, they were rallying to "defend the capital," richly deserved such suspension. "If there ever was," he said, "in any portion of the republic, any spot of earth, or any time, when and where the writ of *habeas corpus* ought to be suspended, the city of Baltimore is the spot, and the last five weeks the time, for its suspension."

Though the war was not inaugurated to destroy slavery, but to save the Union, it could not but happen that questions would arise in which the former would be involved, and concerning which the government, however anxious to avoid it, would be compelled to commit itself to some line of policy. The first question that arose related to the principle that should be recognized in regard to slaves who might escape and take refuge within Union lines. Should they, or should they not, be returned to their owners? There were many in the federal army whose sympathies were with the master rather than with the slave, and who were disposed to return the fugitive to his former owner. To meet the case, notice was given in the Senate on the 4th of December, 1861, by Mr. Wilson, of his purpose to introduce a bill to punish members of the army for arresting, detaining, or returning such fugitives; and, on the 23d, he actually introduced such a bill. During the discussion which ensued, Mr. Saulsbury offered an amendment, making it penal for officers and soldiers to entice slaves from their masters. Mr. Wilson expressed his opposition to the amendment, and "to any legislation protecting, covering, or justifying slavery for loyal or disloyal masters." "What I want to do," he said, "is to put upon the statute-book of this country a prohibition to the officers of the army from arresting, detaining, and delivering up persons claimed as fugitives by the use of military power."

But simply not to return fugitives, it was soon found, failed of meeting both the exigencies of the case and the growing demands of the popular mind. Why these thousands of able-bodied men should not aid in defending and fighting the battles of the Union was a question that clamored for an answer. Nor was Mr. Wilson slow in reaching the conclusion, that here was an element of power that should not remain unemployed, much less be left for the enemy to use. On an amendment to a bill before the Senate concerning the militia, that there should be no exemption "on account of color or lineage," Mr. Wilson expressed his admiration at the audacity and thoroughness with which the Southern leaders carried forward their work of treason, "using every man who could do any thing, no matter how halt or maimed he might be, if he could strike a blow." "We are," he said, "in one of the darkest periods of the contest: and we had better look our position in the face; meet the responsibilities of the hour; rise to the demands of the occasion; pour out our money; summon our men to the field; go ourselves, if we can do any good, and overthrow this confederate power, that feels to-day, over its recent magnificent triumphs, that it has already achieved its independence. Bold and decisive action alone, in the cabinet and in the field, can retrieve our adverse fortunes, and carry our country triumphantly through the perils that threaten to dismember the republic."

Subsequently, during the discussion of the measure, Mr. Wilson reported a bill with fifteen sections relating to this subject. The bill was passed and approved on the 17th of July, 1862; and thus was taken one of those strides in the course of justice to others on which the nation entered mainly in self-defence, — a measure which Senator Saulsbury bitterly denounced as "the most magnificent scheme of emancipation yet proposed."

As the war advanced with at best a varied experience of light and shade, successes and reverses, as the army was wasting away, and the "beginning of the end" did not appear, it became evident that there ought to be not only more vigor infused into its operations, but something more reliable than the system of voluntary enlistments to supply the waste of numbers, and to give confidence to both the army and the nation. To meet this great want, Mr. Wilson reported, from the Committee on Military Affairs, a bill for calling out and enrolling the national forces, and other purposes, in thirty-six sections. In explanation of its provisions Mr. Wilson said, —

"Sir, we have endeavored to frame this great measure for the defence of the perilled nation against the blows of armed treason so as to bear as lightly as possible upon the toiling masses, and to put the burdens (as far as we could do so) equally upon the more favored of the sons of men. It is impossible, in this world of inequality, to frame a measure of this character to bear equally upon all conditions of men; but this bill has been framed in the earnest desire to make its burdens fall as gently as possible upon the poor and dependent sons of toil. But it is a high and sacred duty, resting alike upon all the citizens of the republic, upon the sons of toil and misfortune and the more favored few, to labor, to suffer, ay, to die if need be, for the country. Never since the dawn of creation have the men of any age been summoned to the performance of a higher or nobler duty than are the men of this generation in America. The passage of this great measure will clothe the president with ample authority to summon forth the sons of the republic to the performance of the high and sacred duty of saving their country now menaced, and the perilled cause of freedom and civilization in America, and of winning the lasting gratitude of coming ages, and that enduring renown which follows every duty nobly and bravely done. The enactment of this bill will give confidence to the government, strength to the country, and joy to the worn and weary soldiers of the republic around their camp-fires in the land of the Rebellion."

On the question of who should be exempted from the draft, there was quite a divergence of sentiment. On the motion to exempt the clergy, Mr. Wilson said that he "would not exempt lawyers and clergymen;" though subsequently he offered and supported an amendment that "ministers of the gospel, or members of religious denominations, conscientiously opposed to the bearing of arms, might be considered non-combatants, and be assigned to some other service."

During the last session of the Thirty-seventh and in the Thirty-eighth Congress, Wilson introduced and carried through, besides the above-named, —

A bill to facilitate the discharge of disabled soldiers.

A bill to improve the organization of cavalry forces.

A bill to amend an act for enrolling and calling out the national forces.

A bill to establish a uniform system of ambulances.

A bill to increase the pay of soldiers to sixteen dollars per month.

A bill to provide for the examination of officers of the army.

A bill to re-organize the quartermaster's department.

A bill to incorporate the National Academy of Sciences.

A joint resolution recommending the appointment of wounded soldiers to office.

In the Thirty-ninth Congress, 1866, Mr. Wilson introduced a bounty bill for the benefit of soldiers in the war, which failed to pass; but he was subsequently upon a committee of conference, where he secured an agreement upon the main provisions of the bill reported by him, and they were enacted into the present law.

Gen. Scott, at the close of the extra session, 1861, wrote Wilson a warm letter of thanks for his services, and expressed the opinion that he had done more work at that session than all the chairmen of the military committees for twenty years; and he did it well. Mr. Cameron too, secretary of war, pronounced his services "invaluable."

But the drafting of bills, and making of speeches, and watching measures on their passage, and taking care of them, is only a fraction of the duty of the chairman in time of war. During the four years of conflict, the people went to Washington, many with knapsacks on their backs, and many others with only carpet-bags; but, whether with knapsacks or only bags, a great many of them wanted some attention. Privates wanted to be made officers; officers wanted promotion; men and officers wanted furloughs, or had been bothered about their pay or their rations, or had been abused or neglected by somebody; and they must have the influence of the chairman to get their several cases looked into. Civilians wanted appointments for themselves or their friends in the departments or in the army; or they wanted soldiers discharged because they were minors or *non compos;* or they wanted contracts; or they had some new patent-gun, or Greek fire, or infernal machine, which would end the war in less time than Gov. Seward predicted, if they could only get the generals or corporals of the army to examine them. These folks came down upon him in swarms, — large numbers of them with business that was legitimate enough and should be attended to, but not officially belonging to him. But nearly everybody knew Wilson: he had made a speech in their town, or brother Charles or brother John was personally acquainted with him; and he had, besides, the reputation of being always ready to take up any case of suffering or hardship.

So they were after him day and night, before breakfast and after dinner, on his way to the Capitol or to the War Department, at the committee-room, in the corridors, and everywhere. And then the letters, — the long, illegible, undecipherable, recommendatory, complaining, soliciting, and condemnatory, all sorts and kinds, and all to be attended to, acknowledged, and most of them answered, — these things kept Wilson hard at work long after midnight nearly all the time.

And yet he thought he was not doing enough. We well remember walking with him one evening, after the adjournment, in the Capitol-grounds, and hearing him say that he was ashamed that he was not doing more for the cause, and that he believed he should go home and raise a regiment for the war. A day or two after this, he expressed his firm intention to enter the military service, and started for Massachusetts, where he raised the Twenty-second Regiment, nine companies of the Twenty-third Regiment, one company of sharpshooters, and two batteries of artillery. He went to Washington with the Twenty-second, encamped on Hall's Hill in Virginia, and ultimately resigned the coloneley to Col. Gove, it being the decided opinion of leading men that he could not be spared from the committee and the Senate. The Twenty-second was a very fine regiment; but, in getting it ready, he spent all his money, and ran in debt a thousand dollars in addition. Many of the soldiers of this regiment and the families of those who never came home have since been in distressed circumstances; and no case has come to the knowledge of their first commander without meeting a generous response. We can say with certainty, that no soldier in distress has ever asked from Wilson a contribution that he didn't get, if Wilson had the money. In order to make himself more familiar with the wants of the army and the details of the camp, Wilson joined the staff of Gen. McClellan. This was the largest staff ever seen in Washington; and Wilson learned many useful things while connected with it, which were of use to him as a senator, and member of committee.

CHAPTER XV.

Reconstruction.

THE Thirty-ninth Congr[illegible] which met Dec. 4, 1865, [illegible] one of the most important to the [illegible]ountry and to mankind that ever sat. The armies of the Rebellion had been crushed; slavery had gone down; the rebel States which had been living under the confederate constitution and laws were — they did not exactly know where: and what to do, and how to do it; what to enact in order to secure equal rights to all, black and white; what should be done to prevent another rebellion, without at the same time being harsh and seemingly oppressive to those who had raised the one which had been put down, — these were grave problems. They were much complicated by the condition of parties in the North. Had the people of the North been agreed, much of the difficulty of the situation would have been avoided; for the insurgents would have seen the full meaning of their defeat, and their submission would have been real, while now it was only pretended. They were conquered physically, but, in spirit and language and purpose, defiant as ever. The Democrats of the North kept alive the hope of a re-action in their favor in some of the States; and, when that should come, they could, by the aid of the rebel votes, return to power; and so they encouraged the rebel spirit, and denounced the Republicans as usurpers and tyrants. The effect of this conduct compelled the Republicans to adopt measures for the protection of the Union-men and freed-men, which otherwise would have been wholly unnecessary; and hence all the centralization, and all the acts complained of as tyrannical, came as a necessary consequence of the hostile, defiant, and rebellious attitude of those who had agreed to accept the situation. History will declare that no rebel — officer, private, politician, or citizen — who came in and frankly acknowledged his intention to accord to the colored race the rights that were acquired by the proclamation, and acted accordingly, has ever been refused full and complete amnesty in letter and spirit, or denied any of the rights or privileges, social, moral, or political, that are enjoyed by any of the most favored of the people. The trouble was, they wanted all without making this concession; and whether to grant it or not constitutes the principal practical difference in parties to-day. But the slaves were men now; and, in the absence of any disposition on the part of the dominant white race to do them justice, their rights must be secured by the power that had granted them. The power to grant involves the power and duty to defend; and in this case that power was the nation, and its prerogatives and responsibilities were now in the hands of the Republican party.

Wilson, by the generosity of his nature and by conviction, was in favor of the mildest measures the nature of the case would permit, and give security; and, in many of his speeches before and during the rebellion, was always charitable to the actors, however severely he condemned and denounced the actions. But he did not let his kindly feelings blind him to the necessity of studying the situation, and adopting such measures as would make plain the meaning of the bloody conflict. So much life and treasure must not be expended merely to get things back where they were in 1860.

It will be impossible to give a full account of his connection with measures during this Congress. A hasty sketch must suffice.

In the course of the debate on the Freedmen's Bureau, Mr. Cowan of Pennsylvania, one of those conservative gentlemen of the Republican party who usually voted with the Democrats, and did all they could to demoralize the party and defeat its policy, said, "Thank God, we are now rid of slavery! Let the friends of the negro (and I am one) be satisfied to treat him as he is treated in Pennsylvania, as he is treated in Ohio, as he is treated everywhere where people have maintained their sanity upon the question." This was too much for Wilson; and he rejoined, in that pungent, crisp style for which he is distinguished, as follows:—

"The senator from Pennsylvania tells us that he is the friend of the negro. What, sir, he the friend of the negro! Why, sir, there has hardly been a proposition before the Senate of the United States for the last five years, looking to the emancipation of the negro and the protection of his rights, that that senator has not sturdily opposed. He has hardly ever uttered a word upon this floor the tendency of which has not been to degrade and belittle a weak and struggling race. He comes here to-day, and thanks God that they are free, when his vote and his voice for five years, with hardly an exception, have been against making them free. He thanks God, sir, that your work and mine — our work, which has saved a country and emancipated a race — is secured; while from the word 'go' to this time he has made himself the champion of 'how not to do it.' If there be a man on the floor of the American Senate who has tortured the Constitution of the country to find powers to arrest the voice of this nation, which was endeavoring to make a race free, the senator from Pennsylvania is the man; and now he comes here and thanks God that a work which he has done his best to arrest, and which we have carried, is accomplished. I tell him to-day that we shall carry these other measures, whether he thanks God or not, whether he opposes them or not." (Laughter and applause in the galleries.)

In reply to James Guthrie of Kentucky on the Civil-rights Bill, Mr. Wilson said, —

"The senator tells us that the emancipated men ought to have their civil rights; that the black codes fell with slavery: but the senator forgets that at least six of the re-organized States in their new legislatures have passed laws wholly incompatible with the freedom of these freedmen; and so atrocious are the provisions of these laws, and so persistently are they carried into effect by the local authorities, that Gen. Thomas in Mississippi, Gen.

Swayne in Alabama, Gen. Sickles in South Carolina, and Gen. Terry in Virginia, have issued positive orders forbidding the execution of the black laws that have just been passed. So unjust, so wicked, so incompatible, are these new black laws of the rebel States, made in defiance of the expressed will of the nation, that Lieut.-Gen. Grant has been forced to issue that order which sets aside the black laws of all these rebellious States against the freedmen, and allows no law to be enforced against them that is not enforced equally against white men.

"This order issued by Gen. Grant will be respected and obeyed, and enforced in the rebel States with the military power of the nation. Southern legislators and people must learn, if they are compelled to learn by the bayonets of the army of the United States, that the civil rights of the freedmen must be and shall be respected; that these freedmen are as free as their late masters; that they live under the same laws, shall be tried for their violation in the same manner, and, if found guilty, punished in the same manner and degree.

"This measure is called for, because these reconstructed legislatures, in defiance of the rights of the freedmen and the will of the nation embodied in the amendment to the Constitution, have enacted laws nearly as iniquitous as the old slave codes that darkened the legislation of other days. The needs of more than four million colored men imperatively call for its enactment. The Constitution authorizes, and the national will demands it. By a series of legislative acts, by executive proclamations, by military orders, and by the adoption of the amendment to the Constitution by the people of the United States, the gigantic system of human slavery, that darkened the land, controlled the policy and swayed the destinies of the republic, has forever perished. Step by step we have marched right on from one victory to another, with the music of broken fetters ringing in our ears. None of the series of acts in this beneficent legislation of Congress, none of the proclamations of the executive, none of these military orders protecting rights secured by law, will ever be revoked or amended by the voice of the American people. There is now.

'No slave beneath that starry flag,—
The emblem of the free.'

"By the will of the nation, freedom and free institutions for all, chains and fetters for none, are forever incorporated in the fundamental law of regenerated and united America. Slave codes and auction-blocks, chains and fetters and bloodhounds, are things of the past; and the chattel stands forth a man, with the rights and powers of the freemen. For the better security of these new-born civil rights, we are now about to pass the greatest and grandest act in this series of acts that have emancipated a race and disinthralled a nation. It will pass, it will go upon the statute-book of the republic, by the voice of the American people; and there it will remain. From the verdict of Congress in favor of this great measure no appeal will ever be entertained by the people of the United States."

This was confident and emphatic language enough, and grated

harshly upon the ears of the Bourbons, who were fancying a tremendous re-action: but the course of the convention at Baltimore on the 10th of July, 1872, shows how true was the statement, and how well Senator Wilson foresaw and comprehended the nature of the controversy and its results. Cowan and Hendricks could little imagine then how laboriously they were working to build up an embankment which they would so soon travel to Baltimore to help destroy.

We approach now a point where Senator Wilson found it his duty to stand in opposition to Mr. Sumner on a question relating to the most judicious method of securing the rights of the colored race. The joint committee of fifteen, of which Mr. Fessenden was the head on the part of the Senate, and Thad. Stevens on the part of the House, brought forward a proposition to amend the Constitution by submitting to the States a new article: viz.: "Representatives and direct taxes shall be apportioned, among the several States which may be included within this Union, according to their respective numbers, counting the whole number of persons in each State, excluding Indians not taxed; provided that, whenever the elective franchise shall be denied or abridged in any State on account of race or color, all persons of such race or color shall be excluded from the basis of representation." The purpose of this amendment was to secure suffrage to the freedmen; but, in order to amend the Constitution, the amendment must be framed so that three-fourths of the States will vote for it. As the people of the States have always had the right to fix the franchise to suit themselves, and were very jealous of any infringement of that right by Congress, it was known to a certainty that a proposition to give the elective franchise to the freedmen would not command the necessary three-fourths of the States; but it was foreseen that every State would desire a full representation, and, to secure it, would allow the colored people to vote in order to have them counted in the basis of representation. The proposition encountered fierce opposition. The Democrats all opposed it because it would secure suffrage to the colored people, who, they said, were unfit to vote; and Mr. Sumner opposed it because it would commit the government to a principle which would exclude them from voting. The Democrats opposed it because it would help, and Mr. Sumner opposed it because it would not help, them. Jack Rogers of New Jersey, a leading Democrat, was greatly excited on the subject, and spoke at great length against the article. Mr. Marshall of Illinois, another of the magnates of the party, and friend of Greeley, declared the proposition "wholly untenable, monstrous, absurd, damnable in its provisions, a greater wrong and outrage on the black race than any thing that has ever been advocated by others." Mr. Nicholson of Delaware said, "If they (the Republicans) shall finally triumph in the mad schemes in which they are engaged, they will succeed in converting that heretofore sacred instrument, reverenced and obeyed till the present dominant party came into power, from a bond of union to a galling yoke of oppression, — a thing to be loathed and despised." The things thus denounced were all indorsed at Baltimore the other day by the Democratic Convention.

Mr. Sumner, however, was the one who set it off in the highest style of condemnatory art. He said, —

"It reminds me of that leg of mutton served for dinner on the road from Oxford to London, which Dr. Johnson with characteristic energy described as bad as bad could be, ill-fed, ill-killed, ill-kept, and ill-dressed. So this compromise is as bad as bad can be; and even for its avowed purpose it is uncertain, loose, cracked, and rickety. It is no better than the 'muscipular abortion' sent into the world by the 'parturient mountain.' It makes the Constitution a well-spring of insupportable thraldom, and once more lifts the sluices of blood destined to run until it comes to the horse's bridle. Adopt it, and you put millions of fellow-citizens under the ban of excommunication; you will hand them over to a new *anathema maranatha;* you will declare that they have no political rights which white men are bound to respect. Adopt it, and you will cover the country with dishonor. Adopt it, and you will fix a stigma upon the very name of republic. As to the imagination there are mountains of light, so are these mountains of darkness; and this is one of them. It is the very Kohinoor of blackness. Adopt this proposition, and you will be little better than the foul harpies who defiled the feast which was spread. The Constitution is the feast spread for the country; and you are now hurrying to drop into its text a political obscenity, and to spread on its page a disgusting ordure,

'Defiling all you find,
And, parting, leave a loathsome stench behind.'"

In reply to these assertions Mr. Wilson said, —

"He profoundly regretted to see indications that the amendment was doomed to defeat. My heart, my conscience, and my judgment, approve of this amendment; and I support it without qualification or reservation. I approve of the purpose for which it is introduced. I approve it because I believe it would sweep the loyal States by an immense majority; that no public man could stand before the people of the loyal States in opposition to it, or oppose it with any force whatever. I approve it because I believe, if it were put in the Constitution, every black man in America, before five years could pass, would be enfranchised, and weaponed with the ballot for the protection of life, liberty, and property."

Referring to the speech of Sumner, he said, —

"We are told that it is immoral and indecent, an offence to reason and conscience. Sir, this measure came into Congress with the sanction of the Committee on Reconstruction, composed as it is of men of individual honor and personal character, and as true to the colored race as any other men here or elsewhere. It comes to the Senate by an overwhelming vote of the House of Representatives. It is sustained by ninety-nine out of every hundred journals that brought the present administration into power; and, were it submitted to the American people, it would, I am quite sure, be sustained by men in the loyal States, who believe that the soldier who fought the battles of the republic is the equal of the traitor who fought against the country. I see no compromise in it, no surrender in it, no defilement of the Constitution in it, no implication that can be drawn from it against the rights or interests of the colored race: on the contrary, I believe the black men from the Potomac to the Rio Grande would go for it, and rejoice to see it adopted. Being incorporated in the Constitution, the practical effect would be this, and only this: it would raise up a party in every one of these States immediately in favor of the enfranchisement of the colored race. That party might be influenced by the love of power, by pride, by ambition. These men might begin the contest; for they would not like to yield the power of their States in Congress: they might begin the battle, animated by no high and lofty motives; but, as soon as the discussion commenced, it would address itself to the reason, the heart, and to the conscience, of the people. The advocates of negro enfranchisement would themselves speedily grow up to believe in the justice, equity, and right of giving the ballot to the black man. There would be discussion on every square mile of the rebel States. Appeals would be made to their pride, their ambition, to their justice, to their love of fair play, to their equity. All the interests and passions, and all the loftier motives that can sway, control, and influence men, would impel them to action. They would co-operate with the friends of freedom thoughout the country. We would give them our influence, our voices, and our aid, in fighting the battle of enfranchisement. They would have the support and the prayers of the poor black men of the South; and, before five years had passed away, there would not be a rebel State that did not enfranchise the bondman."

Referring to the policy of "enlightened Christian States" in refusing the right of suffrage to the negro, he said,—

"After all the fidelity and heroic conduct of these men, prejudice, party-spirit, and conservatism, and all that is base and mean on earth, combine to deny the right of suffrage to the brave soldier of the republic. God alone can forgive such meanness; humanity cannot. After what has taken place, is taking place, I cannot hope that the constitutional amendment proposed by the senator from Maine will receive a majority of three-fourths of the votes of the States: I therefore cannot risk the cause of an emancipated race upon it. In the present condition of the nation, we must aim at practical results, not to establish political theories, however beautiful and alluring they may be."

We imagine that no one can

read this sketch of the debate, and the extracts from the speeches, without realizing at once the sincerity and the practical wisdom of Mr. Wilson. It was indorsed by the people of Massachusetts, and met the approval of the common sense of the nation.

CHAPTER XVI.

What a Working-man has done for Working-men.

UPON the first entrance of Wilson into public life, he began to advocate measures tending to give employment to working men and women, and to open up to them all the chances for advancement which republican institutions afford. To this end, in the town-meetings of Natick, he joined the party which was in favor of providing better houses for the common schools, apparatus, improved books, furnishing text-books to the children of the poor gratis, better teachers, and longer terms, and that wanted the town to buy a farm and a house for the unfortunate and poor. As has been related, in the legislature his first important step was the presentation of a report in favor of the proper division of labor, and the means to enlarge the opportunities for work and the increase of wages. Farther on he advocated the extension of the right of suffrage, and opposed the provision which degrades the man by depriving him of his right to vote when he has been stripped of his property and his health. He was a strong advocate of a provision to compel all corporations to issue stock in small denominations, so that people of moderate means could invest their hundred or their fifty dollars in any business, and share in the profits of the water-power or other manufactories. He has been a strong advocate of homestead acts, of laws exempting from seizure the poor man's furniture and a portion of his wages, of laws abolishing imprisonment for debt, laws to open the public lands to actual settlers, and laws to shorten the hours of labor.

It will be remembered that Congress enacted an eight-hour law for the benefit of the laborers on the public works; but some of the officers in charge of forts, arsenals, and buildings, immediately reduced the pay of the employees in the same proportion as the reduction of the hours. This aroused the sensibilities of Senator Wilson; and on the 29th of April, 1869, he wrote a sharp letter to Hon. John

A. Rawlins, secretary of war, in which he stated the case with great ability, and showed how that construction defeated the intent of the statute. We give the conclusion of this letter: —

"During the debate, I took occasion to say, in substance, that I should vote against Mr. Sherman's amendment, for the reason that I wished to give the eight-hour movement a fair trial; that I thought the government employing a few hundred mechanics and laborers could afford to test the eight-hour experiment; that I was not convinced that toiling men could perform as much work in eight hours as ten hours, or that they would receive as much pay for eight hours as for ten hours; but that it might be for the material, intellectual, and moral interests of the masses of the people, whose lot it was to toil for their subsistence, to reduce the hours of labor; and, if that reduction would be conducive to the interests of laboring-men and laboring-women, it would be a source of gratification to every benevolent heart and every generous mind. I maintained that capital needed no champion in this country and in this age; that we were made for something better and something higher in this country than to pile up a thousand millions annually; that what we wanted to grow in this Christian land was a healthy race of men and women with cultivated heads and hearts and consciences; that whatever tended to dignify labor or lighten its burdens, to increase its rewards or enlarge its knowledge, should receive their sympathy, and command their support; that, animated by these sentiments, I should vote against Mr. Sherman's amendment, and for the bill as it came from the representatives of the people." (Sherman's amendment was, that the rate of wages should be the current rate at the time and place when and where the work was to be done.)

"No senator suggested that the passage of the bill reducing the hours of labor one-fifth reduced the wages of labor one-fifth: on the contrary, all admitted that it reduced the hours of labor without reducing the rates of wages. Mr. Sherman's amendment was intended to reduce the rate of wages in proportion to the reduction of time. Sixteen senators voted for it to accomplish that avowed purpose: twenty-one senators voted against it to defeat the accomplishment of that purpose. The action of the officers of the government is in direct opposition to the declarations of senators, and in opposition to the vote of the Senate. The recent action of the House of Representatives is an emphatic declaration against the construction put upon the law. I think this action of the House should be an admonition to those officers to revise their opinions, and revoke their orders.

"Respectfully yours,

"HENRY WILSON."

In a speech delivered at Faneuil Hall Oct. 14, 1868, he said, —

"To provide for the expenses of that Democratic rebellion, the Republican party were compelled to take the responsibility of arranging a system of taxation; and they so adjusted that taxation as to make the burden bear as lightly as possible on the productive interests of the country and upon the working-men of the country. More than one-half of the duties levied on imports are assessed on wines, brandies, silks, velvets, laces, and other articles of luxury, chiefly consumed by the more wealthy portion of our countrymen. The duties imposed on the necessaries of life — upon tea, coffee, sugar, and other articles entering into the consumption of the masses of the people — are made as low as possible; and discrimination is made in favor of our mechanical and manufacturing industry.

"The Republican party spurns this Democratic doctrine of taxing every species of property according to its value. It believes in discriminating in favor of poor, toiling men, and of putting the burden of taxation on accumulated capital and large incomes. In time of war, when the nation needed money so much, the Republicans exempted nineteen out of every twenty dollars of the incomes of the people. This was done to relieve the working-men, whose small incomes were required for the support of their families and the education of their children. We exempted all incomes under six hundred dollars; and this exemption included the incomes of nearly all the laboring-men, mechanics, and small farmers, of the country. We taxed all incomes from six hundred dollars to five thousand dollars five per cent, and all incomes over five thousand dollars ten per cent. That was not *equal* taxation; but it was *just* taxation; for it was based on the sound policy of putting the burden upon capital, and taking the burden from labor. Now we have taken the tax from all incomes less than a thousand dollars, and we tax all incomes above a thousand dollars five per cent, thus relieving the working-men and nearly all the mechanics and farmers from taxation on incomes. We Republicans intend to stand or fall by this policy, which discriminates in favor of the poor, the mechanics, the small farmers, and the working-men of the country. We serve notice on the Democratic party, on all the supporters of this anti-democratic doctrine of the equal taxation of every species of property according to its value, that we Republicans will never agree to the taxation of the little earnings of working-men at the same rate we tax the incomes of the Stewarts and the Astors, the great corporations and capitalists of the country. We give the Democracy notice that we will never tax sugar, coffee, and tea at the same rates we tax silks and wines and brandies; that we will never tax a gallon of milk as high as we tax a gallon of whiskey. We give the Democracy notice that we will not tax the tools of the mechanic, the horse of the drayman, the little homes and farms of the poor, and the incomes of working-men needed for the support of themselves and the support of their households. We Republicans will never consent to the putting of the burdens of the government equally on the small accumulations of the poor and the great capitals and large interests of the country. That is the position of the Republican party; and it is a position in favor of the productive interests of the nation and the interests of the working-men: and we Republicans mean to stand by it, or fall by it; live by it, or die by it. Every laboring-man in America, every mechanic, every farmer, and every business-man, who desires to develop the mighty resources of this country, and carry it upward and onward in a career of power and prosperity, should spit upon and trample upon this democratic doctrine of equal taxation, which is against labor, and in favor of capital; against the loyal, and in favor of the disloyal, portions of the land."

During the last session of this Congress, 1872, he made a proposition to add two to the number of commissioners to investigate the circumstances of working-people, to obtain statistics and information on the general subject of labor, and to suggest methods for the welfare and promotion of the masses; and he interested himself actively in support of the measure.

The circumstances of Wilson's early life; the poverty of his father; the struggles of his mother to find bread for him and his brood of brothers, and to keep them clothed in decent garments; his hard labors on the farm; his weary and vain search for employment at only moderate wages; his association with other young men striving with himself to become respectable and useful in the world under great disadvantages and slight hopes of success; his study of slavery, and knowledge of the personal deprivations and hardships of the colored race, with which he became cognizant in the flush of youth; and his companionship with mechanics and operatives in mills and shops, — have all tended to keep his thoughts and sympathies with the down-trodden, the poor, and the common people. The prodigious influence of slavery in degrading labor in this country early impressed his mind; and to get rid of that curse and abomination appeared to him to be the first and most immediately important step. That has been accomplished; and the effect of emancipation upon the white race is now becoming perceptible: but the long and arduous labors and anxieties and dangers of Senator Wilson in assisting to that consummation can never be properly recounted and understood. He has made more than thirteen hundred public speeches, a large majority of which were directly in the interests of the people who are doing the world's weary drudgery and necessary work. You can scarcely take one of his speeches, and open it anywhere, that your eye will not see something for the common mass, — encouragement, sympathy, hope, or the defence of their rights, and their claims to manhood and prerogatives. The subject is ever uppermost in his mind, and it comes out on every occasion. He has travelled from one end of the country to the other at all seasons, and many times worked all night for thousands of nights, giving his time, his thoughts, and his earnings to the cause of the poor, absolutely and without stint. Instead of studying law, and putting his splendid abilities into the Supreme Court at the rate of ten thousand dollars the single case, as some have done, to place money in his own pocket, he has defended the rights of the country and of humanity without pay in the higher court of public opinion and popular appeal, and devoted, besides, nearly every dollar of his salary as a legislator, and his pay as an author, which has been handsome, to the relief of the soldier and the unfortunate.

Always and everywhere has he advocated and demanded equality, and a fair chance and a free field for every son and daughter of the race. And perhaps, after all his efforts and labors and trials and successes in his various schemes for the good of mankind, his brilliant example to the youth of America and the world, showing and proving what a poor, obscure, uneducated boy may accomplish when he resolutely takes hold of life in earnest, and perseveringly adheres to a purpose, is the most valuable legacy he will leave to his countrymen. He has assiduously labored to secure for all a chance, and the best chance, to be something; he has urged them to try the experiment; and he has done for himself what he would have them do for themselves.

CHAPTER XVII.

His Work in Congress.

TO convey an idea of the industry, and attention to business, of Senator Wilson, we make a transcript of his part in the proceedings of two or three sessions.

Thirty-ninth Congress.

Reports by Senator Wilson, Nos. 142, 789, 975, 1085, 1134, 1184, 1224, 1238, 1293, 1359, 1498, 1667, 1815, 1867, 1894, 1976, 1992, 1993, 2000. Resolutions 75, 143, 183, 584, 694, 764, 999.

Remarks on the District Suffrage Bill.

Remarks on the bill for the admission of Nebraska.

Remarks on the bill to protect the national cemeteries.

Remarks on the Tariff Bill.

Remarks on the bill to amend the act incorporating Orphans' Home.

Remarks on Bankrupt Bill.

Remarks on claims in insurrectionary States.

Remarks on the Civil Employés Compensation Bill.

Remarks on the bill fixing rights of volunteers.

Remarks on bill for relief of certain drafted men.

Remarks on bill for relief of vagrant children in the District.

Remarks on Military Government Bill.

Remarks on Military Academy Bill.

Remarks on Consular and Diplomatic Appropriation Bill.

Remarks on bill to abolish peonage.

Remarks on Louisiana Reconstruction Bill.

Remarks on bill to extend rations to certain officers.

Remarks on bill to facilitate settlement of paymasters' accounts.

Remarks on bill to establish Department of Education.

Remarks on bill to provide compound interest notes.

Remarks on bill relative to courts-martial.

Remarks on bill relative to soldiers' bounties.

Remarks on bill relative to increase of pay of army-officers.

Remarks on Tax Bill.

Remarks on bill for admitting Colorado.

Remarks on Fortification Bill.

Remarks on Naval Appropriation Bill.

Remarks on Tariff Bill.

Remarks on bill relating to brevets.

FORTIETH CONGRESS.

Bill to fix the number of judges of Supreme Court.

Bill to amend franchise act District of Columbia.

Bill relating to judges of Supreme Court.

Bill to amend National Currency Act.

Bill to amend Tenure-of-office Act.

Bill to reduce the army.

Bill to re-organize the grades of army-officers.

Bill to furnish supplies for Indian Bureau.

Bill to consolidate infantry regiments.

Bill relating to freedmen's hospitals.

Bill to relieve the soldiers who sustained losses by disasters to the steamers "Winfield Scott" and "San Francisco."

Bill to reduce the militia in the South.

Bill to establish a line of steamers to Europe.

Bill to equalize distribution of banking capital.

Joint Resolution to drop from the rolls army-officers absent without leave.

Joint Resolution to re-appoint Louis Agassiz regent Smithsonian Institution.

Joint Resolution donating cannon for a monument to Lincoln.

Joint Resolution for an amendment of the Constitution.

Joint Resolution for information relating to the fisheries secured by the Alaska purchase.

Joint Resolution in reference to establishing a branch of Soldiers' Home on the Pacific coast.

Joint Resolution in reference to management of Freedmen's Bureau.

Joint Resolution for purchase of a collection of war-views.

Joint Resolution calling for a list of pardons for offences against revenue-laws and for counterfeiting.

Remarks on president's message.

Remarks on bill to restore Indian Bureau to War Department.

Remarks on resolution for payment of national debt.

Remarks on bill concerning militia.

Remarks on Pacific Railroad.

Remarks on Copper Bill.

Remarks on bill to provide for reduction of forces.

Remarks on suffrage amendment.

Remarks on governments of Virginia and Texas.

Remarks on Consular and Diplomatic Bill.

Remarks on Joint Resolution for printing medical history of the Rebellion.

Remarks on bill for removing disabilities.

Remarks on Currency Bill.
Remarks on Army Bill.
Remarks on bill to fix status of judge-advocates.
Remarks on bill relating to general of the army.
Remarks on bill relating to additional bounties.
Remarks on bill relating to military instructors.
Remarks on joint resolution to complete Pacific Railway.
Remarks on bill to strengthen public credit.
Remarks on Legislative Appropriation Bill.
Remarks on Post-office Appropriation Bill.
Remarks on Civil Appropriation Bill.
Remarks on bill relating to pay of committee clerks.

The above are in addition to all merely private bills, joint resolutions, and remarks thereon, and incidental remarks.

Forty-first Congress.

Bill to establish lines of steamships.
Bill for more equal distribution of currency.
Bill for relief of Orlando Brown.
Bill relating to freedmen's hospitals.
Bill to relinquish the interest of the United States in certain lands on the Pacific to San Francisco.
Bill to appoint a commission to examine claims of loyal persons for supplies, &c.
Bill to grant two million acres of land for education in the District of Columbia.
Bill to remove disabilities from persons engaged in rebellion.
Bill relating to Freedmen's Bureau.
Bill relating to pensions.
Bill relating to freedmen's hospitals.
Bill to grant an increase of pension to widows of officers.
Bill to remove disabilities of Alexander Rives.
Bill for relief of scouts and guides in Alabama.
Joint Resolution for sale of arsenal at Bergen Heights.
Joint Resolution for sale of Chattanooga Rolling-Mill.
Joint Resolution donating Lincoln Hospital to Columbia Hospital for women.
Joint Resolution relating to retirement of Gen. Heintzelman.
Joint Resolution authorizing the secretary of war to take charge of cemeteries at Antietam and Gettysburg.
Joint Resolution respecting pay of enlisted men.
Joint Resolution for protection of soldiers and their heirs.
Joint Resolution to drop from the rolls certain officers absent without leave.
Joint Resolution donating certain condemned material to the Industrial Home School.
Joint Resolution authorizing the president to make a survey for a ship railway or canal across the Isthmus of Darien.
Joint Resolution calling for copy of contracts for ordnance with Norman Wiard.
Joint Resolution to define the meaning of the eight-hour law.
Remarks on Currency Bill.
Remarks on Pacific Railway, and government interest therein.
Remarks on Resolution for protection of soldiers and their heirs.

CHAPTER XVIII.

Conclusion.

HENRY WILSON has now been presented to the reader in his character as a public man and legislator; and the limits assigned to this work prevent any extended description of his many and important labors in various causes and directions. As an effective campaigner, he has had more experience than any man now living; and his speeches furnish the statistics and the facts which carry conviction to the minds of the sober, reflecting, honest classes of the country, whose judgment is influential, and whose opinions prevail in the small villages and school-districts of the land. In 1857, in the spring, he went to Kansas, and found the free-State men desponding, inactive, and proposing to stand still, and let the enemy have it all their own way. Wilson saw this would not answer; that there must be action: and the people of the Territory, the free-State men, must organize, and make fight. After many days' labor, he succeeded in converting the leading men to his views: and he then came back to Massachusetts, and, by persevering effort, succeeded in raising funds to carry on the campaign in Kansas; and by this means the Territory was saved to freedom.

As an editor and author, Wilson has achieved an honorable success. In 1848 he purchased "The Boston Republican" to advocate in its columns the measures and principles of the Free-soil party; but his engagements on the stump, and in his business as a manufacturer, prevented him from giving to it close personal attention. The mercantile instincts of Boston were then not in harmony with the Free-soil movement; and hence patronage in the way of advertising was not to be had to any amount. Financially the investment was a failure, and he lost heavily.

He has written two volumes on the Antislavery Measures in Congress, and one on the Reconstruction Measures, which are valuable and interesting. His principal work, "The History of the Rise and Fall of the Slave-Power in America," is a work of much larger scope and pretensions; and the first volume, recently published, has received the highest encomiums of the leading critics in the country. "The Albany Journal," "Boston Traveller," "Boston Globe," "New-York Tribune," and most of the principal newspapers in the large cities, have spoken of it as eminently fair, clear, truthful, interesting, well conceived, well executed, and a valuable contribution to our literature. It has drawn special letters of approval from W. H. Seward, William Lloyd Garrison, and other distinguished men.

In boyhood he saw the lamentable effects of the use of alcoholic liquors as a beverage in causing crime, and in keeping the common people in their condition of poverty and degradation; and he early resolved to abandon their use, and do what he could to persuade others to. He initiated the Congressional Temperance Society, and by its agency and influence succeeded, for a time at least, in saving more than one brilliant man of genius from degradation, and their constituents from the dishonor which is brought upon a people through the frailty of representatives addicted to the vice of intemperance. A late disgraceful demonstration at a city in Connecticut provokes comparisons from which we refrain, as the people of the country — those who imbibe as well as those who do not — are able to judge of the propriety and the importance of having in high office and for rulers those only who can command themselves. The following, which we clip from a newspaper, has been the rounds; but it is worthy of a continued circulation, and we forward it on its mission: —

Moral Bravery.

Twenty years ago a young man went to Washington with a petition to Congress from the people of old Massachusetts. While in that city, he was invited to dine with the celebrated John Quincy Adams.

Many great men sat at the table. The young man had been poor, and was then only a mechanic in moderate circumstances. During dinner, Mr. Adams said to him, —

"Will you take a glass of wine with me, sir?"

The young man was a temperate man; but the eyes of many greater than himself were upon him. They were all wine-drinkers, and it was no small matter to decline such a request from his venerable host. No wonder the young man was embarrassed; that he blushed and hesitated. It was a trying moment for him; but he was a true man. He had real manhood, and he stammered, —

"Sir, I never take wine."

Nobly said, young man! Massachusetts heard that answer, and understood it. She saw in Henry Wilson a man that could be trusted; and she made him one of her senators. To-day, as for several years past, he is known as Senator Wilson. God bless him! May our readers follow his example, and, however and by whomsoever tempted, stick to their principles!

In 1868 Mr. Wilson united with the Congregational Church, and since then has given much of his time, talents, and money in forwarding the enterprises of the denomination and of the Church universal.

When Wilson was fairly established in Natick, he brought his father and mother there, that he might aid them and care for them in their declining years; and, notwithstanding his incessant labors and engagements, they were never overlooked or neglected. His wife's mother has for years been a member of his family, and speaks of his devotion as in no wise short of a son's in its warmth and constancy. While he was in Europe in 1871, visiting the places of interest, studying the phases of society, meeting and conversing with the statesmen and with men of science and letters, he let no week pass without writing to his mother-in-law, now more than eighty years of age, and with no property to lead him to expect any return through the kindly remembrance of a testamentary devise.

Among his neighbors there is never a whisper or hint of lack on his part of personal integrity, neighborly kindness, or faithfulness to the great causes whose championship he has assumed.

That he is ambitious none will deny: but the cause of freedom, the welfare of mankind, the elevation of the masses, have never been in the market to be disposed of for the gratification of his personal aspirations; and the making of money out of his positions has never been even alleged against him. Had he not been ambitious, he would not have succeeded.

We do not present Henry Wilson as a perfect man, for he is intensely human; but as an organizer, a peace-maker, a wise counsellor, an efficient legislator, a far-seeing statesman, a dutiful son, and a specimen product of American institutions, we trust the reader will find him in the front rank, and worthy to wear the honors for which he has been designated.

www.ingramcontent.com/pod-product-compliance
Lightning Source LLC
Chambersburg PA
CBHW032014010726
47493CB00007B/2392
* 9 7 8 3 3 3 7 4 0 2 8 8 4 *